S0-BNS-255

You're invited to...

## *Return to Tyler*

Where scandals and secrets
are unleashed in a small town
and love is found around every corner...

Don't miss any of these
special stories!

*Secret Baby Spencer*
Jule McBride
Nov. 2000

*Patchwork Family*
Judy Christenberry
Dec. 2000

*Prescription for Seduction*
Darlene Scalera
Feb. 2001

*Bride of Dreams*
Linda Randall Wisdom
Mar. 2001

Dear Reader,

Harlequin American Romance is celebrating the holidays with four wonderful books for you to treasure all season long, starting with the latest installment in the RETURN TO TYLER series. Bestselling author Judy Christenberry charms us with her delightful story of a sought-after bachelor who finds himself falling for a single mother and longing to become part of her *Patchwork Family*.

In Pamela Browning's *Baby Christmas*, soon after a department store Santa urges a lovely woman to make a wish on Christmas Eve, she finds a baby on her doorstep and meets a handsome handyman. To win custody of her nephew, a loving aunt decides her only resource is to pretend to be engaged to a *Daddy, M.D.* Don't miss this engaging story from Jacqueline Diamond.

Rounding out the month is Harlequin American Romance's innovative story, *Twin Expectations* by Kara Lennox. In this engaging volume, identical twin sisters pledge to become mothers—with or without husbands—by their thirtieth birthday. As the baby hunt heats up, the sisters unexpectedly find love with two gorgeous half brothers.

Next month, look for Harlequin American Romance's spin-off of TEXAS CONFIDENTIAL, Harlequin Intrigue's in-line continuity series, and another WHO'S THE DADDY? title from Muriel Jensen.

I hope you enjoy all our romance novels this month. All of us at Harlequin Books wish you a wonderful holiday season!

Melissa Jeglinski
Associate Senior Editor
Harlequin American Romance

# JUDY CHRISTENBERRY
## Patchwork Family

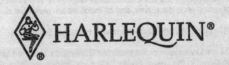

# HARLEQUIN®

TORONTO • NEW YORK • LONDON
AMSTERDAM • PARIS • SYDNEY • HAMBURG
STOCKHOLM • ATHENS • TOKYO • MILAN • MADRID
PRAGUE • WARSAW • BUDAPEST • AUCKLAND

Special thanks and acknowledgment are given to Judy Christenberry for her contribution to the Return to Tyler series.

ISBN 0-373-16853-5

PATCHWORK FAMILY

## ABOUT THE AUTHOR

Judy Christenberry has been writing romances for fifteen years because she loves happy endings as much as her readers. Judy quit teaching French recently and devoted her time to writing. She hopes readers have as much fun reading her stories as she does writing them. She spends her spare time reading, watching her favorite sports teams and keeping track of her two daughters. Judy's a native Texan, but now lives in Arizona.

### Books by Judy Christenberry

**HARLEQUIN AMERICAN ROMANCE**

*4 Brides for 4 Brothers
†Tots for Texans

## Who's Who in Tyler

*Quinn Spencer*—His prowess in the courtroom is rivaled only by his skill in the bedroom.

*Molly Blake*—Her new Breakfast Inn Bed caters to lovers—but her own bed is empty....

*Sara Blake*—She wants a daddy for Christmas....

*Martha Bauer*—A master quilter with a sweet tooth...and a soft heart.

*Ursula Wilson*—Nothing gets past this old biddy, on Ivy Lane...or anywhere in Tyler, for that matter.

*Emma Finklebaum, Tillie Phelps, Bea Ferguson, Merry Linton and Lydia Perry*—Tyler's Quilting Circle—they sew the most beautiful quilts...and matchmake the most unlikely couples.

*Marge Phelps*—The proprietor of Marge's Diner, where good food is served up along with plenty of gossip.

*Kaitlin Rodier*—The keeper of Kaity's Kids, Tyler's premier day care center.

*Elias Spencer*—This patriarch watches after his sons... but has a wandering eye for the ladies.

*Brady Spencer*—He doctors broken bones and broken hearts...all except his own.

*Seth Spencer*—The first of the Spencer brothers to fall... Will he be the only one to wed?

# Chapter One

Blood pumped through Molly Blake's body as she raced across the town square of Tyler, Wisconsin.

"You're being ridiculous!" she panted to herself as she ran, but she didn't slow down. Instead, her mind listed the reasons for panicking.

Thank God, it wasn't a large town square. It wasn't a large town, for that matter. But if she'd had to run any farther, she might have collapsed.

She leaned for only half a second by the discreetly lettered brass plate that read Trask and Spencer, Attorneys-at-law. With a prayer of hope, she drew a shuddering breath and shoved away from the red-brick wall of the building and slammed back the door to the law offices.

Warmth flooded her. After all, it was winter in Wisconsin, the beginning of December. Every occupied building had its heat on full blast. And she was still wearing a knitted cap over her messy long braid, still had her navy pea jacket wrapped around her, her gloves on her hands, boots on her feet.

She shivered. The cold was coming from deep within her. From her fears. From—

"May I help you?" a pleasant woman asked.

In the almost shadowy interior of the building, Molly hadn't really seen her.

Gasping for air, Molly got out, "I need to see Mrs. Trask, at once. It's—it's an emergency!"

With the calm precision of someone who loves routine, the woman asked, "Are you a client of Mrs. Trask's?"

Molly wanted to leap over the desk and yank the woman to her feet by the elegant lapels of her gray suit, even though she couldn't blame the secretary for her lack of enthusiasm. Molly knew she wasn't at her best.

She'd run a few brief errands at the post office and the grocery, after dropping off her child at day care. She'd planned to hurry home to continue refinishing one of the wooden tables she'd bought for the dining room. The stained sweat suit beneath her coat wouldn't do her any favors in the impression department, either.

"Yes!" she said, drawing out a hiss as she fought to control her temper.

"Your name and the nature of your business?" the secretary prodded.

Dear God, she might throttle the woman yet. "Molly Blake. And I'll explain the nature of my business to Mrs. Trask. Just tell her I'm here and it's an emer—"

"I can't do that, Ms. Blake."

"Why not?"

"Because she's out of the office."

"What?" Molly almost screamed, unable to retain any semblance of sanity. If she didn't get help, she wouldn't be sane, anyway. If there was no hope—

Just as the woman began to caution her for her

unruly response, a door to the left of the reception desk opened and a handsome man stepped out.

"Problem, Mrs. Allen?"

Molly had seen him before. Heard stories about him. Overheard him explain with great clarity his distaste for children. She wanted nothing to do with Amanda Trask's partner, Quinn Spencer.

Anyway, he wouldn't understand.

"Yes, sir," the secretary said, nodding her head like a bird considering a worm. "This lady seems a bit overheated."

"An amazing feat in this weather," the lawyer drawled.

Molly's dislike instantly turned to hatred. How easy to be above it all with a wealthy family, a secure job, a life of—of jet-setting!

She drew a deep breath and faced Mrs. Allen. "When will Mrs. Trask be available?"

Surely she had made that request in a calm, professional manner. Why was the woman hesitating?

It took a nod from the attorney for the secretary to open an appointment book on her desk.

"I believe she's free on the eleventh...of January," the woman said. She looked up at Molly over the rims of her glasses, pen in hand. "Do you want that appointment?"

"No!" Molly cried, pain filling her voice and her body. By then it would be too late. Too, too late. "I can't wait," she gasped, reduced to pleading. "Please, if you'll talk to Amanda, I'm sure—"

"I don't believe we've met," the man, Quinn Spencer, murmured.

Molly stared at him, shock making it difficult to even figure out what he'd said. He wanted to do the politically correct niceties when she was dying here? With a nod, she turned back to the dragon guarding the entrance to the secret cave. "Please—"

"I'm Mrs. Trask's partner. Did you say you're a client of Amanda's?"

"Yes," she snapped.

Before she could again plead for help, he spoke to the secretary. "Mrs. Allen, if you'll pull Mrs. Blake's file and bring it into my office, I'll see if I can assist her, since she said her visit is an emergency."

She might not like what she knew about Quinn Spencer. She might have decided thirty seconds ago she hated him. But she did know everyone considered him to be a brilliant attorney. Any port in a storm, as her dad had always said.

"Thank you," she muttered, and hurried into his office as he held the door for her.

QUINN SPENCER CLOSED the door behind him even as he considered Amanda's client. Had he made a mistake, agreeing to see her? He'd heard her name— maybe Amanda had mentioned it—but he couldn't quite put together what business the woman was conducting with his partner.

She'd seemed nearly hysterical, but at least she didn't seem dangerous at the moment.

And he was considerably larger than she. His solid six feet weren't exceptional in Tyler, but he had a good seven or eight inches on her. And in spite of the bulky coat, he suspected she'd have trouble weighing more than one-hundrd-and-ten pounds.

She was still standing, her face tight, her body tense.

"Sit down, Mrs. Blake. Take off your coat. It's too warm in here to be all bundled up." He could do the manners thing. A lot of times it helped ease the situation, whatever it might be.

"Please! You don't understand!" She waited until he circled his desk. Then she began pacing his spacious but pleasantly cluttered office as if she were in a psych ward unit. Wringing her hands. Frowning fiercely. Well, as fierce as a five-foot-four blonde with big blue eyes could seem.

"No, but I will if you'll stop pacing and explain it to me."

He didn't win any brownie points for his calm demeanor.

"I'm going to lose everything! I can't— I've budgeted very carefully! It's— I can't! I won't let that woman—"

There it was again. That raw emotion, the pain, the anger. Not the first time he'd heard those things, but there was no question she was feeling them all.

He softened his voice. After all, he'd dealt with distraught women before. Sometimes the emotional reaction had even been caused by him. This time he was sure he was innocent.

"So your difficulty stems from your budget?" After all, that was the only clue she'd given him.

"No!" she said, whirling around to face him. Anger became the dominant emotion. "No! My difficulty stems from that damned Ursula Wilson!" Then she looked stricken, a guilty expression on her lovely lips.

Uh, not lovely, he stuttered in his mind. He hadn't meant to notice that. He turned his attention to whatever had changed her expression. "What's wrong?"

"I shouldn't have said that."

He blinked twice before he asked cautiously, "You mean it's not true? Mrs. Wilson isn't—"

"Yes, it's true! She's trying to get revenge for— Anyway, it's true, but I shouldn't have cursed her."

He almost laughed out loud. In all her ranting, the woman was castigating herself because she'd said "damn?" He couldn't believe it. Wisconsin was known for its wide-eyed milkmaids, but this was ridiculous.

Covering his hand with his mouth and pretending to cough, he suggested again, "Why don't you sit down and give me the details of Mrs. Wilson's activities? I'm slightly acquainted with her and have some knowledge of local law, so..." Inside he was smirking. Some knowledge of the local law. Yeah. Local, state, national *and* international.

Suddenly, as if he'd discovered the key to unlock all the information stored inside, she did as he asked, almost falling into one of the leather wing chairs in front of his desk and spewing out information.

"She's trying to block me from getting my business license. She's also filed a zoning protest! I've done everything exactly as is required. I've met every deadline, paid every fee. I talked to the Chamber of Commerce. I even talked to Joe and Susannah Santori and the Kelseys. I've done everything I could possibly do! But she won't—"

"Whoa!" Quinn said, even holding up a hand, the universal symbol of stop, afraid his voice wouldn't penetrate her spate of words. "Let me be sure I've followed everything so far. Uh, just for the record, what kind of business are we talking about?"

"My bed-and-breakfast. Breakfast Inn Bed on Ivy

Lane.'' The tiniest measure of pride appeared in her words, along with all those other emotions.

Well, that information cleared up some of his questions. Ursula Wilson lived on Ivy Lane. A neighbor. Joe and Susannah ran the only bed-and-breakfast in town. Mrs. Blake's competition. And the Kelseys had a boardinghouse.

"Okay, you're starting up a business. You've done everything you're supposed to do, and you feel Mrs. Wilson is trying to shut you down?''

"Yes!''

"She's filed something at Town Hall?''

Hesitation had her blinking those big blue eyes. "I—I'm not sure. Lydia said—''

"Lydia?''

"Lydia Perry. She said Mrs. Wilson is circling a petition among my neighbors. And—and she said she was going to prevent the zoning change.''

He made a couple of notes. Lydia Perry was a member, albeit a fairly new one, of the beloved Quilting Circle that operated out of Worthington House. Quinn's favorite people.

"When did she tell you this?''

"This morning! I was in the grocery picking up a couple of things and she stopped me. Said she'd been meaning to call me. I—I tried to remain calm, but my heart started beating fast and I couldn't breathe and—and I left her standing there and ran over here. You see, I need to— It has to succeed. I've got enough to make it for a year. New businesses need that much cushion. I know that. I've planned for it. I've been fixing up the house, buying furniture. I've even bought some quilts, so I can— Never mind, you don't need to know that. But I have to succeed! And

I will not allow that woman to destroy everything I've worked for just because she's jealous!''

"Take a deep breath," he counseled in his most charming, soothing, masculine, I-know-best manner, hoping to relieve some of her stress.

Instead, it appeared he'd pressed the wrong button. She leaped to her feet and leaned over his desk. "Weren't you listening? Remaining calm isn't going to get me anywhere. I've got to do something! I need to know what I can— I need to see Amanda!" she exclaimed, and turned to charge the door.

He stayed in his chair. "She's out of town and won't be back until next week. There's an emergency case that requires—"

"*I'm* an emergency case!" she reminded him.

"Yes, you are, and that's why I'm talking to you. I understand the urgency, Mrs. Blake. But if you've given yourself a cushion of a year, as you've said, then another half hour for me to understand the problem, whereby I will be able to plan our moves, doesn't seem too much to ask."

SHE HATED HIM.

The calm, rational man, making her sound like an overemotional woman. Okay, so she couldn't deny either of those assessments. But he didn't understand how difficult the past two years had been. How much she had resting on the hope of the bed-and-breakfast.

He didn't understand about Sara, her beloved daughter. She couldn't fail Sara. Not when Christopher had already abjectly failed his daughter. Not when Sara had no one else to depend on.

Drawing a deep breath, she tried to bring her emotions under control. After all, Mr. Spencer had at least listened to her so far. And if she lost everything—she gulped back a sob—then she'd find a way. She'd move back to Chicago, get a regular job again.

She and Sara would survive, no matter what.

A calm centered in her and she took her seat again. Looking up from the clenched hands in her lap, she said, "I beg your pardon, Mr. Spencer, for my rudeness. You're quite right, of course."

He stared at her as if she were an alien creature. She couldn't blame him. She had a feeling she hadn't made the man's day with all her weeping and wailing and gnashing of teeth.

He smiled, another of those I-can-charm-your-socks-off smiles that made her want to slap him. Christopher had practiced those—on a lot of women. Except her, of course. He hadn't needed to charm *her*.

"Thank you for—for calming down, Mrs. Blake."

He'd been about to say for coming to her senses. She knew it. She hated him.

"Certainly. Do you believe you'll be able to help me resolve these issues?"

"Of course we will. We're a well-respected firm, and for good reason. If, as you say, you've done everything you should, Mrs. Wilson won't have a leg to stand on. Now, I just have a couple more questions."

"Yes?" Okay, that had been a little short, less gracious. She tried again with a smile that she hoped looked better than it felt. "Of course. Please, what else can I tell you?"

"You could explain your remark about revenge."

She closed her eyes briefly, hysterical laughter rising in her. Fighting it back, she cleared her throat and said, "I hope you'll excuse my emotional outburst earlier. Those remarks really had no place— I'm sure Mrs. Wilson's reasons are based on—"

Quinn folded his hands together and leaned forward, interrupting her stammering explanation. "Mrs. Blake? I understand that your feelings are not facts. It's my job to evaluate the situation. But I need to have your impressions. All of them."

He was right as usual, logical, calm. She definitely hated him. With a deep sigh, she avoided his gaze and abruptly began, "My husband, Christopher, is— was a native of Tyler, Mr. Spencer."

She got more reaction that she expected. "You're Christopher Blake's wife?"

That question was the first non-lawyerly remark the man had made. Molly proceeded with caution. "Widow. I'm his widow. Did you know my husband?"

She already knew the answer. Christopher had spoken of Quinn Spencer occasionally, usually with bitterness because Christopher didn't have the fortune to back him that Quinn had. It made being a playboy so much more difficult. Playboy on a budget. No, somehow that just didn't work.

"Of course I did," Quinn replied. "We went through school together. I wasn't aware that he'd died. When—"

"Two years ago." She couldn't be that gracious. And she couldn't be remorseful. She'd tried, but the grieving widow role required more talent than her amateur acting skills.

When she said nothing else, he prodded, "And this applies to Mrs. Wilson because..."

She licked her dry lips. "It applies because Mrs. Wilson hates my guts. She envisioned her daughter, Layla, Linda, Lannie, I don't know, some L name, as Christopher's wife."

He shielded his mouth again, giving another polite cough. "I believe her name is Lila."

She shrugged her shoulders, tired of the story. "Whatever. It seems her daughter married beneath herself because she still loved Christopher and I had stolen him, according to Mrs. Wilson." How she wished she'd been able to give him back.

"I see." Very lawyerly. He even nodded, steepling his hands beneath his chin.

Very nice hands. Large, strong, well cared for.

She jerked her gaze away. It immediately collided with his. A question resided in his hazel eyes. Or were they green?

What was wrong with her? The man's eye color had nothing to do with her.

"Do you have other questions?" she asked, seeking that peaceful calm, the center of the storm that had gotten her through the past few minutes.

He stood, giving her a polite smile. "No, not at the moment. I'll study your file. Then I'll check with the clerk's office to see if Mrs. Wilson has filed."

"There's a petition. She's circulating a petition to all my neighbors, trying to get them to side with her, to keep me from opening." How could she have forgotten—

He looked down at his notes. "I believe you did mention it. We won't be able to stop her petition, but we should be able to come up with a strategy to counteract it. A petition isn't legally binding, you know. It's a tool for persuasion. But there are others."

She took another deep breath. She was verging on the hysterical again. Determined not to ruin her performance of a calm woman, however pathetic it had been, Molly stood. "Yes, of course. I didn't mean to repeat myself." She extended her hand, trying to be professional. However, as she realized she'd removed her gloves at some point in their conversation, she also noted the brown stains on her fingers.

"Oh!" she exclaimed, snatching her hands behind her back. "I'm sorry. I'm staining some furniture and—"

"That's quite all right," he assured her soothingly.

Except it didn't soothe her. She whirled toward the door, anxious to escape the most humiliating experience she'd ever suffered through.

"Your coat, Mrs. Blake?"

It was getting worse. Not only had she taken off her gloves, she'd apparently shrugged out of the old navy pea jacket she'd found in one of the closets and fallen in love with. The pea jacket that covered the stains on her sweats.

After all, she'd intended to make two stops that would take five minutes, tops, and then be back at work. It seemed silly to even think about changing.

Wrong.

"I—I'm sorry. I know I look a mess. I'm staining a table—"

"Yes, I believe you did say that. Don't concern yourself, Mrs. Blake. This isn't New York. We don't have a dress code for our clients."

Gracious answer. So why did it make her want to scream? Maybe because he was standing before her in a very expensive navy pinstripe suit and leather wing tips that would probably cover her food budget for half a year. His light brown hair, with just a touch of blond to suggest days spent in the tropics, had been expertly cut. Businesslike, of course, but with a touch of freedom, giving him a sophisticated air of self-determination. The perfect jet-setter cut.

Christopher would've loved it.

She shrugged on her coat without responding.

Then, sticking her hands into her coat pockets, she nodded to the man with impeccable clothes. Impeccable manners. Impeccable everything.

"I appreciate your time, Mr. Spencer. Your secretary has my address for billing. I'll look forward to hearing from you."

As an exit line, it wasn't bad. Until she neared the door and almost tripped over a table holding an expensive vase.

She grabbed the vase and stepped back. Then, after taking a deep breath, she steadied it back in its place.

Without turning around, offering another apology or trying for a better exit line, she walked out of the office.

And prayed Amanda would get back to town at once.

## Chapter Two

"Good afternoon, ladies," Quinn said, his best smile in place. "Are you keeping warm?"

The quilting circle of older women smiled back at him, as welcoming as ever. Each lifted her cheek for the kiss he always bestowed on them, patting his arm as if he were a little boy.

Maybe that was the charm that frequently brought him to Worthington House. To the rest of the world, he was a playboy. To the ladies here in this sun-drenched room that looked out on a cold world, he was Quinn, a young lad with a good heart.

Or maybe, he reluctantly admitted to himself, these ladies were his surrogate mothers, making up for his mother walking out on her family so many years ago. His friends would laugh at the thought that Quinn Spencer longed for his mother. Or any woman.

He'd been only seven years old when his mother, Violet, had left them. They'd been in Tyler only six months, his father having relocated from New York where he left behind his lucrative career on the stock exchange for a quieter, gentler life in the small town. Elias had hoped his high-strung wife would learn to relax once she was out of the bustle of the city, but Violet couldn't—or wouldn't—change. She'd run off with Ray Benedict, her lover from New York, much to the shock of their social circle in the city and the residents of Tyler. Not to mention her husband and three sons.

"We didn't expect you today, Quinn dear," said Martha Bauer, one of the older members, calling Quinn back from his memories. She patted an empty chair next to her. "Sit down."

"I'd love to as long as you share your M&M's," he teased. Martha had a sweet tooth and he kept her supply of candy well stocked.

Tillie Phelps nodded her head. "We even have cookies today. Bea made a fresh batch this morning."

Bea Ferguson, at sixty-seven, was one of the younger members. She blushed but nudged a plate toward Quinn.

"Don't mind if I do, Bea. These look terrific." And they were. He enjoyed them more than any expensive hors d'oeuvres he'd ever been served.

As he munched, he watched the ladies set tiny stitches in the colorful quilt they were making. Each quilt was either given to charity or sold and the money used to help the community. The women had become legendary both for their incredible artistry and their hearts of gold.

"Where is this one going?" he asked, while he considered how to bring the conversation around to the reason for his visit.

Merry Linton, another newcomer to the group, smoothed a loving hand across the patchwork quilt. "It's lovely, isn't it? It's called Bachelor's Puzzle."

He nodded, still tangling with his own puzzle.

Bea answered his question. "That lovely young woman with the new bed-and-breakfast has purchased it."

He choked on a cookie crumb. Clearing his throat, he asked cautiously, "Do you mean Molly Blake?"

Martha and Tillie exchanged a look he couldn't interpret, but it put him on his toes. Something was up.

Martha smiled. "Why, yes, dear, have you met Molly? Isn't she wonderful?"

Quinn frowned. He could agree that Molly was attractive. Wonderful? The distraught, angry woman he'd faced in his office that morning was hard to fit into the simple word *wonderful*.

Complex, challenging, sexy. He shook his head. No, not sexy—

"You haven't met her?" Tillie asked, obviously interpreting his shake of head as a no.

"Yes, yes, I have. This morning, in fact. So, you like the idea of a new bed-and-breakfast?"

"Oh, yes," Emma Finklebaum said with a sigh. "Such a lovely idea. A romantic bed-and-breakfast. And she's going to plan the decor of each suite around one of our quilts."

"Ah," he said, like Sherlock Holmes uncovering a vital clue. "You're glad because you'll make money!"

The ladies chuckled. Through the years, they'd expressed amazement at the rising value of their efforts.

"It's more than that," Martha said. "She's a lovely person...and the best mother in the world."

"Mother?" That subject hadn't come up in their visit that morning.

"Oh, yes," Merry agreed. "Her little Sara is a charmer. Molly brings her to visit us sometimes."

"Sara likes my candy," Martha added, as if that were a vital piece of information.

Quinn smiled, charmed by Martha's pride. He wouldn't tell her that every kid liked candy. He would never do anything to make Martha feel less important than she did.

Tillie, who had remained silent until now, asked, "Why did she come to see you? Is there a problem?"

At her question, all the ladies stopped plying their needles and stared at Quinn.

He held up a hand. "Client confidentiality," he murmured, then waited quietly for their response. He wasn't disappointed.

"Ursula!" Bea exclaimed.

"I can't believe she's still causing difficulties," Merry exclaimed.

But, then, sweet Merry never believed the worst of anyone.

Emma leaned even closer. "What's the problem?"

Quinn carefully phrased his question. "I wondered if any of you had been approached about signing a petition."

"Of course we have!" Martha exclaimed, adding a snort of derision. "That woman thought we'd want to sink poor Molly's plans. As if we would!"

"Why does she want to stop the opening of the bed-and-breakfast?" he asked.

Tillie leaned closer. "She *says* it's because the business will destroy the peace and quiet of Ivy Lane."

"But you don't believe her?"

"Of course not," Bea, unusually animated, replied. "She thinks Molly stole Christopher from her Lila, don't you know."

"As if he were a prize," Emma added.

Quinn tried to picture Christopher as the answer to a woman's dream. In particular, Molly's dream. He'd been trying to do so ever since Molly had left his office.

"And he wasn't?"

The ladies all looked at one another. Finally Martha responded. "No, Quinn dear, he wasn't. He was a selfish, egotistical man. A playboy!" She put all her disgust into her last words.

Quinn cleared his throat. "I'm considered to be a playboy, too," he reminded her.

Martha leaned over to pat his cheek. "But we know better, dear."

Quinn smiled but shook his head. Maybe that was why he loved these ladies. They saw him through a proud mother's eyes. Instead of a mother who'd obviously been so unhappy she'd run away and left her three sons—with no word for over twenty-three years.

"Do you think the neighbors will go along with Ursula?" he asked.

All the women proclaimed their hopes that Molly would come out on top.

Emma capped off their remarks with, "Ursula needs to get a life!"

Such a flippant, with-it comment from eighty-year-old Emma brought a smile to Quinn's face. "I believe you're right, ladies. And I'll see what I can do to help things along."

Amid their praise, he eased himself from the room, promising to visit them again soon.

Heading back to the office, he thought again about what he'd discovered. Ursula Wilson had filed a request to deny the zoning change necessary for Molly's inn, as he'd suspected. She had another week to supply the city with her petition. It needed one-hundred names. In the morning, he had an appointment with the mayor to discuss the potential problem for Molly Blake.

He thought the situation was a tempest in a teapot, but he wanted to be sure to cover every aspect. The passion in Molly Blake's voice prodded him to be thorough.

The woman had intrigued him all day. She'd been a mess, of course, in appearance. But an intriguing mess. A woman who took charge of her future. He'd been impressed with her planning, her hard work.

Then he'd discovered she was a mother.

Any interest disappeared with that information. He'd promised himself never to be involved in a child's life. It was too great a responsibility. One his own mother had abdicated. And he was her son.

MOLLY STARED AT HERSELF in the mirror.

She couldn't believe the difference a few hours had made. When she'd reached the street, after her interview with Quinn Spencer, she'd seen her reflection in a plate-glass window. She'd already realized her appearance was less than professional.

But the physical evidence of her reflection shook her.

All along she'd planned to update her appearance, knowing it would be an important part of marketing her bed-and-breakfast. But she figured that part of her plan could wait. There was no urgency.

Seeing herself as Mr. Spencer must've seen her, however, changed her mind.

The Hair Affair, the beauty salon on the corner, became her immediate destination. Forget the table waiting at home. She had more important business to conduct.

Now she stood before a dressing room mirror, wearing navy wool slacks topped by a cream turtleneck sweater, her hair feathered around her face. The new short style made her feel younger. The manicure gave her a touch of elegance.

She closed her eyes, seeing Quinn Spencer staring at her, respect and awe in his expression. Then she burst out laughing. Talk about fantasy!

The saleswoman in Gates Department Store, the Neiman-Marcus of Tyler, asked in bewilderment, "Is something wrong?"

"Not at all, Mrs. Bell. You've been very helpful. These clothes are exactly what I had in mind. I'll take them. And also the other two pair of slacks. And the blue sweater."

The lady beamed at her. "Excellent choices. You have such wonderful taste."

Probably not what Quinn Spencer would say, Molly admitted, but at least the next time she encountered the worldly Mr. Spencer, she wouldn't feel like Little Orphan Annie.

After she'd paid for and collected her packages, she realized she had almost an hour before she needed to pick up Sara from her friend Kaitlin's day care. Instead of heading for Ivy Lane and home, she went to Worthington House.

The quilting ladies had become a refuge of support and love for Molly. With no family of her own, she'd discovered among them a sweetness and friendship that went a long way to counteracting the anger and bitterness of Ursula Wilson.

"Good afternoon, ladies," she called out as she entered the room where the quilting took place. She always marveled at the women's patience and hard work.

"Molly!" several exclaimed, smiles on their faces. Then they took a second look.

"Why, don't you look pretty!" Martha exclaimed.

Merry beamed at her. "So young and fresh!"

Molly smiled at them. "Well, certainly better than I've been looking lately. I was so involved in fixing up the house, I forgot to fix me up!"

Emma Finklebaum asked, "What made you get all polished up today?"

Molly felt her cheeks heating up. She certainly wasn't going to mention Quinn Spencer. Besides, she'd intended to improve herself all along. "Um, I decided I needed a more professional appearance to sell the idea of my bed-and-breakfast. After all, Ursula is trying to convince everyone I'll be a failure. I didn't want to help her."

Tillie patted her hand. "Good thinking. I think you've made the right decision. Besides, you look so pretty!"

"You certainly do," Bea seconded, causing Molly's cheeks to redden even more. "Why, you might just attract a young man with that pretty smile of yours, don't you know."

Molly's breath caught in her throat and she cleared it before she answered. "Um, no, I don't think— I'm too busy with my plans to— I have no interest in men."

Lydia Perry came in at that moment to distract her friends. Molly breathed a sigh of relief.

"Molly, dear, I'm so sorry I upset you this morning," the lady said as she sat down.

"Oh, no, Lydia, it wasn't your fault," she hurriedly assured her. "I should've remained calm but— but I had no idea Mrs. Wilson had gone so far in her anger."

"But did you see Amanda Trask? Did she tell you what to do?" Lydia persisted.

With all the ladies anxiously awaiting her answer, Molly couldn't avoid mentioning the one man she wanted to forget. "Amanda is out of town, but I spoke with her partner. He's going to look into it."

The ladies exchanged glances and Molly wondered what they were thinking.

Bea nodded. "You can trust Quinn. He's the sweetest boy."

"And very smart," Martha assured her.

"Such a dear," Merry added, a gentle smile on her lips.

Tillie agreed. "He's quite popular around here."

Molly tried to fit the Quinn Spencer she knew, or rather knew about, with the ladies' comments. But the playboy, womanizer, jet-setter and all-around man-about-town just didn't seem "sweet" to her. "I've heard he's a very good attorney."

"Of course he is," Martha said, patting her hand. "Don't worry, dear, he'll take care of you."

Somehow, the thought of letting Quinn Spencer "take care" of her left Molly breathless.

"It's—it's just until Amanda returns. She should be back in town soon." She hoped she didn't sound as edgy as she felt.

If the ladies' satisfied nods were to be believed, she must've have sounded like she had every confidence in Quinn Spencer.

Maybe she was a better actress than she'd thought.

QUINN LEFT THE MAYOR'S OFFICE the next morning, a satisfied smile on his face. The mayor had assured him the entire council was in favor of the bed-and-breakfast. Even if Ursula Wilson got the one-hundred signatures on her petition to bring it before the council, the zoning change would be approved.

He paused on the sidewalk and took a deep breath. It was one of those perfect winter days that occasionally came along, bright sunshine making everything sparkle in spite of the cold air.

Assuring himself that he was only doing so to better serve Amanda's client, Quinn turned in the direction of Ivy Lane. A brisk walk would be good exercise, and he could personally inform Molly Blake of the good news.

He hadn't been down Ivy Lane in a while. It was a stately avenue, lined with old homes built years ago. When he reached the Blake home, he noticed the outside of the home had been recently painted and restored.

"That must've cost a pretty penny," he muttered to himself, remembering Molly Blake's comment about her budget. At least she'd prepared for what was important. A sudden curiosity filled him about the inside. He'd visited Christopher's home once or twice when they'd been in school. Even then the house had been showing its age.

He trod up the steps and crossed the wide porch to rap on the door. A new door, with a delicate stained-glass oval depicting flowers. With a smile on his face, he prepared himself to greet Molly Blake as the door swung open.

Shock rattled through him.

Gone was the harried, frustrated, angry woman with the messy appearance. In her place was a fashionably dressed young woman with pale blond hair feathering around her face, setting it off like a prized picture in a frame. She was dressed in trim wool pants and a blue sweater that enhanced her eyes.

He assumed the worried look on her face was the result of concern about her future. Hurriedly beginning his explanation, he was shocked again when she scarcely acknowledged his words. When she even began closing the door on him, he put out a hand to stop her.

"Wait. Do you understand, Mrs. Blake?"

"Yes, I—" She broke off as a wail floated down the stairs. She gasped and abandoned the door. "I'm coming, sweetie," she called as she raced up the stairs.

Quinn frowned as he found himself standing alone in the entryway. He could leave. But then, if he did, he wouldn't know what was wrong. Not his business, he argued with himself, but he didn't leave.

Instead, he closed the door and stepped toward the stairs. Before he could ascend, Molly came back into sight at the top of the stairs, carrying a bundle in her arms.

"Is everything all right?"

She appeared surprised to find him still there. "No, my daughter is ill. I appreciate what you've done. I'll—I'll call later to discuss it. But she needs me right now."

Quinn had kept his distance from children. And mothers. Too often, he'd seen a woman's selfish disregard for her child's needs. He knew how important the bed-and-breakfast was to Molly.

But not more important than her child.

A moan drifted up from the bundle in Molly's arms. He hadn't realized she was holding her child. She tightened her arms and murmured soothing words.

"She must be tiny," he said with a frown, somehow drawn to the invisible child. "Have you taken her to the pediatrician?"

"I called. He can't see her until late this afternoon."

Quinn could tell she was trying to remain calm, but he heard the panic in her voice. "Is she running a fever?"

"Yes. It's very high."

He stepped even closer and pulled back the blanket, revealing a small face, quite similar to her mother's, with the same pale hair and big blue eyes. "Hello there," he whispered.

The little girl tightened her hold on her mother.

Okay, so he'd never been good with children. Never wanted to be good with children. But he couldn't quite bring himself to walk away from this duo.

"Want me to call my brother?"

Molly blinked those big blue eyes of hers several times before she asked, "Why?"

"Sorry, I forgot you wouldn't know. My brother Brady is a doctor at Tyler General. He might be able to see her now."

He'd offered women gifts before, even occasional

favors, but he'd never seen such intense gratitude in response. She even reached out to grasp his lapel.

"Oh, yes, please. With her fever so high, I'm— I'm worried."

He patted her hand and asked for the phone. She led him to the small desk beside the staircase, standing beside him as he called, cuddling her daughter.

"Dr. Spencer, please. It's his brother, Quinn."

He covered the receiver and said, "They have to go get him."

She nodded, hope in her gaze.

"Brady? It's Quinn. I need a favor. A—a friend has a little girl running a high fever. The doctor can't see her for seven or eight hours. Could you take a look at her?"

His brother's hurried agreement had him hanging up the phone at once. "We need to get her there in fifteen minutes. Do you have a car? I walked."

"Yes! Thank you! Thank you so much. My keys are in the kitchen. I'll just—"

"Give your little girl to me," he ordered, reaching out his arms.

She hesitated, as if not sure she should entrust her precious bundle to him, but then she handed over the child.

Quinn felt the heat rising in waves from the child and understood Molly's fears. The child was very hot. He smiled down at the miserable face. "We're going to take you to the doctor, and he'll make you feel better."

She whimpered and ducked her head against him. He cuddled her closer, surprised at the protective feelings that filled him.

Molly returned, shrugging into her coat. She

scooped the little girl out of his arms and handed him the keys, all at the same time. "You drive, please."

His eyebrows rose. "You want me to drive your car?" he asked, not sure he'd understood.

She nodded as she turned to lead him through the kitchen to the garage. "Yes, please. I have to hold Sara."

Such motherly devotion filled Quinn with stark terror.

# Chapter Three

All Molly could think about was Sara. She murmured soothing words to her daughter as Quinn Spencer drove them to the hospital. Sara had never been sick, other than occasional sniffles, in her four years of life. It unnerved Molly to see her baby in such straits.

"She's so hot," she muttered, scarcely aware she had spoken out loud.

"I'm sure Brady will be able to help her," Quinn assured her. He pulled into the emergency parking area and came to a stop.

Molly was out of the vehicle, Sara still clutched to her chest, before he could come around and assist her. "Will your brother meet us here, in the emergency room?"

"Yes. He should be waiting."

Molly scanned the medical personnel as they entered the hospital. It didn't take her long to identify Brady Spencer. His hair might be darker than his brother's, but they had the same eyes. Besides, he was hurrying toward them.

"Is this my patient?" he asked, voice filled with gentle reassurance. "What's her name?"

"Sara," Molly told him, but she was reluctant to release her child, even to the doctor.

"Hello, Sara," Dr. Spencer said, pulling back the cover to see her daughter's face. "How about we see if we can make you well again? Want to come with me? I may even have a lollipop for you."

Sara nodded. The doctor scooped her from Molly's arms. Molly reached out as he moved away, afraid to lose sight of her daughter.

Strong arms came around her. "She'll be all right, Molly," Quinn whispered in her ear. "You can trust Brady."

With a strangled sob, she instinctively turned into those strong arms and buried her face in his chest. All she could think about was her precious child.

It had been so long since she'd had anyone to lean on, to share her burdens. The comfort the attorney offered was too tempting. She remained there, absorbing his strength, until other feelings invaded her concern.

She jerked herself from his embrace, embarrassed. How could she think about a man, any man, when Sara was ill? She certainly wasn't a lonely widow looking for some man to rescue her. No! She and Sara were a team. They didn't need anyone.

But, for a minute, she admitted, having someone to lean on had felt good.

"I'm sorry. I don't usually fall apart, but Sara's never been really sick and—and—"

"It's all right. I guess I'd feel the same way if my child—" He broke off and looked away from her.

She already knew he had no children and never intended to be a father. One night at Marge's, the local diner, she'd overheard a conversation not intended for her ears. Quinn had been explaining to his companions how he felt about children.

"Children only complicate your life and take up time. I'm always on the go. I'll leave raising the little rug rats to other people," he'd said with a laugh.

Which made his assistance today impressive.

"I appreciate your help. High fever always frightens me." He must think her a real fraidy cat. After all, yesterday she'd been just as frantic. "You must think I'm always— I mean, yesterday—"

He took her arm and drew her over to a row of chairs. "Special circumstances, Molly. Don't worry about it."

She sat down because she didn't know what else to do. She'd wanted to follow the doctor into the examining room, but that hadn't appeared to be an option, which worried her even more. A nurse had hovered at the doctor's side, ready to assist him, and Sara hadn't put up any resistance. Now, Molly clutched her hands tightly together, tensely waiting for the doctor's —and Sara's—reappearance.

A large hand reached out and covered her two. Its warmth helped ward off the chill that was racing through her. "It'll be all right," Quinn whispered.

"I appreciate your talking your brother into seeing us right away. I don't know what could've caused such high fever. It could be meningitis, or even—" she gasped at the thought "—even leukemia."

"It's probably nothing more than the flu, which I've heard is going around."

"You don't know that!" she snapped, refusing to be consoled.

He squeezed her hands and said, "No, I don't, but

we don't want to borrow trouble if it's not necessary."

She closed her eyes and drew a deep breath. "No, of course not. I'm sorry."

He seemed to take her apology in stride. "Do you have any family, other than Sara?"

She shook her head.

"Your parents?"

She stared at him. Did the man think she could carry on a normal conversation when her baby was desperately ill? "They're both dead. My mother died when I was twelve, my father three years ago." Before he could ask, she added, "I was an only child."

As Sara was and would be. Molly had no intention of ever considering matrimony again, of giving Sara a stepfather who might fail her as miserably as her own father had done. No, it would be just the two of them.

"No aunts, uncles, cousins?"

"Are you asking who to notify in case of an accident? Or—or a death?" she demanded, her voice rising.

"No! I was just making conversation," he assured her, squeezing her hands again.

She snatched her hands away from the warmth that had begun to seep into her tense body. Denying herself that comfort made her feel closer to her daughter.

"Molly, I wasn't—" Quinn began, but he halted as Brady appeared, holding Sara in his arms.

Molly exploded from the chair and raced to meet her daughter. "What is it?" she asked the doctor. "Is she okay? What caused the fever?"

"She's going to be fine," Dr. Spencer assured her. Molly's knees suddenly went weak. She would've sagged to the floor if Quinn hadn't been behind her to support her.

It was Quinn who followed up with questions. Molly couldn't speak. "What caused the fever?"

"The flu. It's going around. She got dehydrated, which only made the fever worse."

"I tried to get her to drink juice, but it kept coming back up," Molly told him.

"I know. I've given her a shot that will settle her stomach and ward off any additional infection, and we put an IV in her. I want you to get some Pedialyte to give her. It comes in liquid and Popsicles. She should be able to keep that down. Wash her face with a lukewarm washcloth to help keep the fever from getting too high."

Molly nodded even as she reached for her child. Sara snuggled against her mother, but her eyes never opened.

"Is she asleep?" Molly asked, alarmed.

"Almost. The shot made her drowsy. She needs lots of rest and liquids. Feed her soup, keep her still and call if anything worries you."

"Yes. Yes, of course, Doctor. Thank you so much for seeing us. I can't tell you how much I appreciate—"

Brady Spencer grinned. "Thank my baby brother. He's the reason I worked Sara in. But I'm glad I did. She needed attention right away."

Molly nodded again, swallowing a huge lump in her throat. "Yes, I've already told him how much I appreciated his offer to call you."

The loudspeaker blared out Dr. Spencer's name, and he excused himself, rushing down the hall to his next emergency, leaving Molly holding Sara close.

QUINN WAS RELIEVED at his brother's diagnosis. Molly's fears had begun to affect him, and he'd feared that the small child might've had a dangerous ailment.

She was so tiny. Like a doll.

He offered to carry her, but Molly refused. "I have some money in my purse. Could we stop by the pharmacy here in the hospital and see if they have what the doctor recommended?"

"Yes, of course." He paused and then said, "In fact, why don't we put you and Sara in the car. I'll go back and get the medicine. She'll get heavy if you hold her while we shop."

"Do you mind?" she asked, her blue eyes anxious.

"Not at all." He escorted her to the car, putting her in the back seat, guessing she wasn't going to give up holding her child.

"I'll hurry," he promised. Then he returned to the hospital.

In the pharmacy, he found Pedialyte in clear liquid form and in fruit flavors. And the Popsicles, encased in plastic, waiting to be frozen. He chose some of each variety, wanting to be sure Molly had what she needed. After paying, he hurried back to the car.

"I forgot to give you money," Molly said at once as he slid behind the wheel.

"That's okay. I'll add it to your bill." He'd do no such thing, but those words kept Molly from protesting.

When they arrived back at her house, he came around the car and reached for Sara.

"No! I'll carry her."

"Molly, she'll have to be carried upstairs. Your

arms are probably already tired from holding her. It'll be safer if I carry her. You can go ahead and turn down the covers on her bed.''

''It's on the third floor,'' she warned, watching him.

So much for his manly appearance. She didn't seem to think he could make it that far. ''I think I can make it up two flights of stairs carrying your little girl. She hardly weighs anything.''

As if she took his words as a criticism, she said, ''I try to tempt her to eat. She doesn't have much of an appetite.''

''I think she's small-boned,'' he said, hoping to appease Molly. Hell, he didn't know what four-year-olds should weigh.

He didn't know anything about kids. And didn't intend to. Today was the exception to the rule. He couldn't have abandoned Molly and Sara when he found them in such desperate straits.

She unlocked the front door, waited for him to enter and then pulled it closed behind him to keep out the cold. ''This way,'' she said, circling him and starting up the stairs.

He watched her race ahead of him, her trim figure in his face as he followed. He'd been right about her figure beneath that tacky sweat suit she'd worn yesterday.

She was a very attractive woman.

But she was also a mother.

Cross her off the list of potential lovers.

Too bad.

They reached the second floor and she led the way to a staircase almost hidden in the back of the house behind a closed door.

"Isn't it a pain, living on the third floor?"

"No, it keeps us in good shape."

He couldn't disagree with that statement.

"And it's like living in a tree house. We feel safe, tucked up here."

They reached the top of the stairs and she led him down a short hall, opening the first door on the right. He followed her, seeing only the bed. She pulled back the covers and turned around to take Sara from his arms.

He let the warm little bundle go, reluctantly. It was only because he felt responsible for her, he quickly assured himself. As he stepped back, he took in his surroundings. Not a large room, but it was the perfect child's room. A window seat, partially hidden by pink curtains, graced one wall. There was a mural on the wall next to the hall.

The bed had a pink ruffle around the bottom, beneath a pink and green quilt. Stuffed animals sat on several shelves, as well as storybooks. In one corner at the edge of the matching green rug sat a big brown bear.

A room full of loving touches. He had no doubt about who was responsible for the perfect child's room. Molly Blake was the best mother he'd ever met.

Not that he'd met many mothers. There had been a few society women, a couple of whom had even tried to seduce him when he was dating their daughters. Their selfish attitudes only reinforced his own experience. His mother apparently had been more interested in her own happiness than any problems he or his brothers might have at having been abandoned by her.

Molly was different.

He began backing out of the room. "Um, I'll leave you to make Sara comfortable."

She whirled around. "I can't thank you enough. Oh! The Pedialyte! It's still in the car."

"I'll go get it." He was glad for a real excuse to escape the nest Molly had created.

He hurried down the two flights of stairs and went out to the car. When he'd gotten the large sack, he turned back to the house. As he stepped inside, he drew a deep breath and took in his surroundings for the first time.

The first floor reflected as much love and care as Sara's room. The wood on the banister gleamed with polish. The walls had been recently painted a soft cream. Flowers were tastefully arranged on the desk beside the stairway. A glimpse into the other rooms that opened off the main hall, the living room on the right and a large dining room on the left, were filled with antiques as polished as the banister.

Had she done all the work herself?

It reminded him of the idea he'd intended to explain to Molly. From his own memories of the house, he knew he had the right idea.

But the sudden need to escape, to get out of Molly's personal space—and even the entryway was a reflection of Molly—seized him. He looked around for a place to set the bag.

"Thanks for getting it out of the car for me," Molly called as she came down the stairs.

He jerked around and stared up at her.

"Sara's gone to sleep. She's resting much better and she's not as hot." She reached the bottom of the stairs. "Can I offer you a cup of coffee? It's not much after all you've done for us but—"

"No! No, thank you. I've got appointments," he said, thrusting the bag in her arms. "It was nothing, actually. I hope Sara gets better soon."

And he ran out of the house.

Molly stood there, the bag in her arms, staring at the door through which Quinn had fled.

What was wrong with him? She'd offered a cup of coffee. That was all. You'd think she'd tried to seduce him.

LYDIA PERRY RUSHED OUT of the cold into the warmth of Worthington House early the next morning, knowing she'd already find her friends hard at work on another quilt. They'd finished the Bachelor's Puzzle for Molly Blake yesterday afternoon.

"Have you heard?" she said as soon as she entered the room.

"Heard what?" Martha asked, barely looking up from her stitching.

"About poor little Sara Blake."

Those words got everyone's attention.

"What wrong with Sara?" Merry asked anxiously. The child was a favorite with all the ladies, but Merry especially delighted in her visits.

"She's got the flu."

"Oh, the poor baby," Tillie crooned.

"She had a very high fever. If it hadn't been for Quinn, I don't know what would've happened."

Emma looked up sharply. "Quinn? What does he have to do with Sara being sick?"

All the stitching stopped as the ladies stared at Lydia.

"He called Brady and then took Sara and Molly to the hospital. Sara was dehydrated. He gave her an IV and fixed her up. This nurse I know told me how concerned Quinn was. He stayed with Molly the entire time Sara was with the doctor, holding her hand."

Martha and Tillie stared at Lydia, then at each other, a light dawning in their eyes.

"Do you think—" Tilly began.

"It's possible," Martha agreed, nodding vigorously.

"I can't believe it," Emma protested. "Why, he steers clear of women like Molly. You know that."

"Molly's so pretty," Bea said timidly.

"Did I miss something?" Lydia asked, puzzled by the conversation flowing around her.

"Not really," Martha said, taking up her needle again.

"Now wait just a minute. I brought you the news. You should tell me what you're talking about."

"She's right," Tillie agreed. "It's just that— Well, there's not really anything to tell. More like a hope, don't you know."

"A hope for what?" Lydia asked in frustration.

Martha took up the explanation. "Quinn is a lovely man. Most people think he's a flirt, a playboy, but he's just afraid of being abandoned. That mother of his left him and his brothers afraid of commitment."

"You sound like one of those ladies' magazines, like—like *Cosmo*."

"I know what I'm talking about," Martha said sturdily, determination in her voice. "We want him to be happy."

"He seems happy to me," Lydia said.

"But he's not. The boy hurts. He hides it, but I know," Martha assured her.

"But how does that have anything to do with little Sara?"

"Woman, think with your heart, eh?" Emma suggested.

"You mean you think he and Molly— But if he avoids women like her, I don't see—"

"He didn't avoid her yesterday, according to you," Merry reminded her. "He has such a soft heart."

"He was kind, but that doesn't mean he'll see her again," Lydia pointed out.

"And so? Whose side are you on?" Martha demanded.

Lydia stared at her friend. "Why, yours, of course. And Molly's. I want Molly to be happy. Those Spencer boys, I don't care what you say, they're heartbreakers. Like their pa."

"What do you know about Elias Spencer?" Emma demanded.

Lydia's cheeks turned bright red. "Nothing! I've seen him a few times. About town." Her fingers twitched, telling her friends she wasn't being totally honest.

"Elias suffers from the same problem as the boys. He's never forgiven that woman for leaving him and his sons. Probably never will. Anyone messing with him is asking for heartbreak."

"Then why plan on Quinn having anything to do with Molly? You want her to be heartbroken again? I think Christopher Blake already did enough damage to poor Molly and her little Sara."

"Quinn wouldn't hurt either of them. All we have to do is make sure they spend time together," Tillie said, narrowing her eyes as if trying to think of a plan.

"That won't be a problem," Martha said calmly.

Her friends all stared at her.

"What do you mean?" Lydia asked.

"Just wait and see," Martha said, stitching again. "Are you ladies going to help or just sit there with your mouths open?"

# Chapter Four

The next day was Saturday, so Quinn was able to justify not calling Molly Blake. After all, he didn't conduct business on weekends. No one expected him to do that.

So he could avoid the lady without admitting his reasons for not calling to tell her the good news he'd stopped by her house for yesterday. Or to tell her the idea he'd come up with. Or to see how little Sara was feeling.

When his brother stopped by the family home Saturday afternoon, where Quinn lived, he asked, "Have you heard from Molly Blake?"

Brady raised one eyebrow, staring at him. "No. Why would I?"

Quinn shrugged, trying to look disinterested. "I thought maybe she'd call you if Sara didn't get better."

Shoving his hands into his pockets, Brady leaned against the kitchen counter. "Why wouldn't she be better? You think I didn't make the correct diagnosis?"

"Hey, I wasn't insulting your skills," Quinn hastily assured his brother. "I just thought—"

"Have you called Mrs. Blake?"

"No. Why would I?" Quinn demanded, taking a step back, repeating his brother's words without even realizing it.

"Do what?" Elias, their father, demanded as he entered the room.

Quinn almost groaned aloud. He certainly didn't want either his father or brother to think he had any interest in a woman like Molly Blake. "Nothing."

"I asked why he hadn't called Mrs. Blake," Brady explained, grinning at his brother.

Quinn knew Brady was teasing him. He ground his teeth in silence.

"Who is Mrs. Blake?" Elias demanded. When Quinn had moved back to Tyler over a year ago, he'd returned to his father's house because he didn't have enough enthusiasm for life to find his own place. Somehow his father had interpreted his moving in as a return to the parent-child relationship.

"Dad, it doesn't matter," Quinn hurriedly said.

"She's the mother of a sick little girl. Quinn called me yesterday and asked me to see her."

"This Molly Blake?" Elias demanded.

"No!" Quinn exploded. "Her child, Sara. She's— she's like a doll, tiny, sweet..."

"How old is she?" Elias asked, a frown on his face.

"Four."

"You're interested in a four-year-old?"

Quinn drew a deep breath and scratched his forehead. Finally he stared at his father. "I was concerned about Sara's health, that's all. Anyone would've been. She was running a high fever."

"And so? Why didn't you call this Molly Blake and ask her how the child was feeling?"

"Dad, you don't need to— Never mind. I thought Brady might have heard from her, that's all." Quinn started for the door. He didn't want to answer any more questions about Molly Blake and her daughter.

"What's she look like?" Elias asked Brady.

Quinn spun on his heels and charged back into the room. "No! No, Dad. This isn't a man-woman thing. It's nothing personal. She's one of Amanda's clients and I was trying to help Amanda."

Brady shot him a sly grin. "A real looker. Blonde."

"Hmm, I like blondes," Elias said, staring at Quinn.

"Then *you* call her!" he snapped, and rose to get out of the kitchen before the speculation could go any further.

Unfortunately, he didn't escape. His oldest brother, Seth, and Cooper Night Hawk, a longtime friend and local deputy, came in.

"Hi, guys, glad you're all here," Seth said. "Don't leave, Quinn."

Quinn frowned. He wasn't in the mood for a family moment. He had too much on his mind. "What?"

"Cooper has some news."

That got everyone's attention. A while ago Seth had asked Cooper to find out whatever he could about their mother, Violet Spencer. Now that he was married and had a child on the way, Seth had felt a need to know whatever became of his mother. He'd asked his father if he'd object, but Elias had approved of the search.

Elias leaned forward. "About your mother?"

Quinn returned to the table and fell into a chair.

Everyone's gaze shifted to Cooper.

"Yeah, Mr. Spencer. I'm sorry, but she's...she's dead."

Seth came to stand beside his father, placing a comforting hand on his shoulder. "There's more, Dad. Brace yourself."

"She died in childbirth," Cooper said, after receiving a nod from Seth. "Over twenty-two years ago."

"What?" Brady said, leaping to his feet. "She was pregnant?" He turned to look at his father.

Elias shrugged his shoulders. "She wasn't pregnant when she left us. Probably she and—and that man—" It was as if he couldn't bring himself to even mention the name of her lover. He sighed. "It was a long time ago."

Cooper cleared his throat. "Violet had the baby—and passed on—seven months after she left. Ray Benedict, the man she— Her— Anyway, he died recently. I need to know if you want me to find the child, a girl." Instead of looking at Elias, he let his gaze travel to each of the brothers. "After all, she is your half sister."

"I say yes," Seth said instantly.

"The baby didn't die during childbirth?" Brady asked.

"No."

Brady looked at Quinn, and then Seth. "I agree with Seth. I think we should find her."

Quinn stared at everyone. They had a sister? A child his mother conceived with another man? Renewed anger filled him at her betrayal. But he couldn't disagree with his brothers. They needed closure. Maybe this unknown sister would give it to them. He nodded his agreement.

THE DIFFERENCE IN SARA in just three days was dramatic. By Monday morning, she was racing up and down the stairs in spite of Molly's efforts to keep her in bed.

"I'm all better, Mommy," Sara assured her.

"Just to be sure, come have a snack," Molly tempted, putting a cup of hot chocolate with marshmallows on the kitchen table, along with a muffin.

"First, I has to get Button," Sara said, naming her favorite bear, as she ran out of the kitchen.

Molly sighed. Getting Sara to sit down was like trying to catch lightning in a bottle. Her little girl never seemed to stop. But today Sara would take a nap, Molly decided, her lips tightening, even if she had to sit on the child to keep her in bed.

After lunch, she convinced Sara to go to her room and let her mother read her a story.

"But it's not bedtime."

"I know, but Miss Kaitlin has you lie down on your blanket and rest, doesn't she?" Kaitlin Rodier ran Tyler's day care center, Kaity's Kids, a combination preschool and child care facility.

"Yes," Sara admitted, her bottom lip pushing out a little further. "I shoulda gone to school today. Jeremy will miss me."

"I'm sure he will, sweetie," Molly agreed, pushing a strand of hair behind Sara's ear. Jeremy was Sara's best friend at preschool. "But we have to be sure you're well. We don't want to make Jeremy sick, do we?"

Sara put one little finger at the corner of her

mouth, as she always did when she was thinking. Finally she shook her head no. "I don't want Jeremy to be sick."

"Good. You rest and listen to the story. On Wednesday, we'll go see the doctor and be sure you're well. Then, if he says it's all right, you can go back to school."

"Okay," Sara agreed with a sigh, her eyes slowly closing.

Molly picked up one of Sara's favorite books and opened the page.

"Will that nice man carry me again?"

Molly's head jerked up. "The doctor?"

"No, the man who carried me up here. It was kind of like having a daddy, wasn't it, Mommy? Daddies carry their little kids, don't they?"

Molly struggled to hide the pain that assailed her. "Yes, daddies carry their little kids, sweetie. But Mr. Spencer isn't a daddy. He was just being helpful."

She hadn't even realized Sara had been awake enough to know Quinn Spencer had carried her. She certainly didn't want her daughter thinking of Quinn Spencer as a father image. While the man couldn't be much worse than Christopher, he probably wasn't much better, either.

Playboys never were.

Halfway through the book, Sara was sound asleep.

After dropping a soft kiss on Sara's forehead, Molly put away the book and tiptoed from the room.

Just as she reached the hallway leading to the kitchen, the phone rang. With a gasp, she raced through the kitchen door to grab the phone before it could ring again and awaken Sara.

"Hello?" she answered, her breath shortened.

"Molly? I mean, Mrs. Blake? Is everything all right?"

Quinn Spencer. He probably thought she was going to fall apart again. She took a deep breath. "Everything's fine. I didn't want the phone to awaken Sara. She just went down for her nap."

"How is she doing? Is she better?"

He actually sounded concerned. She decided it was part of his routine, charm any female within a hundred yards. But *she* wasn't susceptible.

"She's much better, thank you."

"Good. Have you taken her to your doctor?"

"We have an appointment for Wednesday afternoon."

"Ah. That's wise."

"Yes. Thank you for calling to check on her."

Before she could hang up the phone, he spoke again. "Wait! I came by Friday morning to tell you I talked to the mayor about your problem. He said he felt sure the zoning change Ursula is protesting will probably pass. All the councilors are in favor of your business."

"Oh! Oh, thank you, Mr. Spencer. I appreciate your assistance."

"Don't hang up. I have an idea that might improve your situation."

"You do?"

"You needn't sound so incredulous, Mrs. Blake," he muttered.

"I apologize," she said hurriedly. "What idea?"

"I thought you should have an open house, invite your neighbors, the town leaders, anyone else with power, to see the changes you've made. I can remember how that house looked when Christopher's mother lived there. You've made a lot of difference. I think your neighbors would be impressed."

Molly was stunned. "I hadn't thought of that. Do you really think it would help?"

"Yes, I do. And invite Ursula."

"What?" She couldn't believe what she was hearing. Invite that woman into her home?

"Let her see what you've done. It probably won't change her mind, but you never know."

Molly swallowed, her mouth suddenly dry. "I'll think about what you've said, Mr. Spencer. And thank you for calling me to give me your favorable report."

"You're welcome. And tell Sara I'm glad she's feeling better."

"Yes, thank you."

She hung up the phone, relieved that her future looked hopeful. But she was also disturbed. She'd just lied to the man.

She had no intention of saying anything to Sara on his behalf.

"YOU STILL HAVEN'T TOLD US your plan," Lydia protested on the next Friday afternoon. "It's going to be Christmas before you know it."

"What's wrong with Christmas?" Martha asked. "You got something against it?"

"Of course not! But I was hoping Molly and little Sara might not have to be alone then. It's difficult to spend Christmas without any family."

"Even I can't act that fast," Martha muttered.

"I guess you're right," Lydia agreed, her shoulders sagging. "I was hoping for too much."

"That doesn't mean we've given up," Emma chimed in.

"We haven't?" Lydia asked, perking up.

"Of course not," Martha reassured her just as the door opened and Quinn Spencer walked in.

"How are my favorite ladies today?" he asked, a smile on his face. He rounded the table greeting each of them.

"We're better for seeing you, my dear, don't you know," Martha said, patting his arm. "I'm so glad you could stop by."

"You know I would never ignore a request from you, Martha," Quinn said. "What's wrong? Is your stash of candy low?" He pulled a bag of peanut-and-chocolate candy from his coat.

She eagerly took them. "Thank you, but no, that's not why I asked you to come by. We need you to do us a favor. I know how busy you are, but I thought on your lunch hour you could run an errand for us."

"Sure." While he spoke, he surveyed their work. "You've started a new one?" he asked, referring to the quilt they were now working on.

"Yes," Emma said. "We do them in sections, you know. We don't just work on one quilt straight through."

He nodded, smiling at her. "I remember."

Martha touched his hand. "See those two quilts? They're king-size, which makes them very large and heavy. We need to get them to Molly, but none of us are strong enough, and she's too little to manage on her own. I wondered if you'd deliver them for us? She's just a few blocks away."

They all saw his hesitation, unusual for Quinn when they asked something of him. Several glances were exchanged, but not Martha's. She sat stitching, supreme confidence on her face that Quinn would accommodate her.

"Um, it's a busy day, Martha, but I can hire someone to take care of that for you. I can see where they'd be a problem."

Martha looked at him briefly, allowing surprise to show on her wrinkled face. Then she reached out and patted his hand. "That's all right, dear. We can hire someone. It was just— Well, you know how sentimental we are about our quilts. I wanted them to be specially delivered, but... I'll call the grocery store and get a couple of their package boys to— No, no, they might not have clean hands."

"We could call the hardware store. Some strong young men work there," Emma suggested.

"Or maybe—" Beatrice began.

"Never mind," Quinn interrupted. "I'll take care of it. I can shift some things."

"Oh no, dear," Martha said. "We don't want to interrupt your busy schedule. We're just grateful you can make time to come see us occasionally. We don't want to—"

"You old fraud," Quinn teased, his voice husky. "You know I wouldn't miss coming to see you." He leaned over to kiss her cheek again.

"Such a sweet boy," Martha said as she patted his cheek, her voice full of love.

His cheeks flushed, Quinn moved over to the quilts. "I'll take care of these right now, so don't worry about your precious delivery. They'll arrive safe and sound."

After the door closed behind him, Martha winked at her friends. "And so what will be our next step?"

THIS WAS A GOOD THING, Quinn assured himself.

When you fear something, it grows in proportion to your fear. Fear gives the enemy power.

He wasn't going to give any more power to Molly Blake. What a ridiculous thought, that he, an international lawyer, well-to-do, respected and admired, feared Molly Blake.

Pulling into the driveway of her house, he parked his car and opened the trunk. Because of their size he carried the quilts one at a time to the front porch.

He was about to use the brass knocker when he took note of the design in the stained-glass oval. Since the bed-and-breakfast was located on Ivy Lane, the design used ivy, its curling tendrils encircling the oval. Then, where it met at the bottom, the ivy entwined itself around two flowers, a red rose and a yellow tulip in the center. He grinned. That block of Ivy Lane was intersected by Rose Street on the south end and Tulip Street to the north. Very nice. He'd heard his brand-new sister-in-law, Jenna, was doing some artwork for Molly. He wondered if she had anything to do with the design.

He brought himself back to the business at hand. Time to make his delivery and get the hell out of there. The brass knocker fell heavily against the door, making a satisfying, sturdy sound.

Little feet hurrying to the door alerted him to Sara's arrival. She tugged the door open about six inches and pressed her face through the opening. In spite of himself, he was glad to see that the child was all right.

He cleared his throat, ready to make his explanation, when he was surprised by her response.

With a beaming smile, she pulled the door wide-open. "Hi, Mr. Man. Did you come to take me to the doctor? I'm all well."

She obviously remembered him. "Uh, no, Sara, I didn't. And I'm glad you're all well. You look lovely today." And she did. Her delicate features, big blue eyes and soft blond hair made her look like a perfect doll. Except she was dressed in sturdy jeans and an open corduroy shirt over a Sesame Street T-shirt.

"Thank you." She reached out, took his hand and tugged. "Come on!"

"But—" He could've resisted, of course, but Sara's excitement and beaming smile was a lure he didn't want to deny. So he followed her willy-nilly down the hall, realizing, as he did so, that they'd left the front door standing open.

Sara raced around the desk beside the stairs to a door on the left, out of sight of arrivals. Pushing it, she tugged him into a big kitchen, brightened by the afternoon sunshine, scented by whatever Molly Blake was baking.

Of course his gaze fixed on the larger version of Sara. She was bent over one of the ovens, her rounded bottom covered in snug-fitting jeans.

"Look, Mommy, Mr. Man is here!"

Molly spun around, almost losing her balance, a startled look on her flushed face. "What— Sara, did you open the front door?"

Quinn watched as the little girl's pleasure disappeared, her eyes widening and one finger rising to her rosebud mouth. "Uh-oh."

Molly composed herself, taking her attention from her child after giving her a warning look. "My apologies, Mr. Spencer, I wasn't expecting— Did you need to talk to me? If you'll return to the living room, I'll tidy up and be right in.''

She was covered with a big white apron that had a few stains on it, and a streak of flour stood out against her red cheek. Maybe it was the smell of whatever was baking, but Quinn found himself thinking she looked delicious.

She gestured toward the door, one eyebrow raised.

"Uh, no! I mean, I don't need to speak to you."

She seemed taken aback by his forthrightness. "Oh. Then why are you here?"

"Martha asked me to deliver the quilts, since they're heavy."

He'd expected a polite thank-you. Instead, surprise followed by excitement filled her beautiful face. Then she rushed past him, followed by Sara, and he found himself standing alone in the big kitchen.

Shaking his head, he turned to follow. Did the woman ever remain in control? Every time he'd seen her, her emotions had been driving her. At least today they were happy emotions.

Since they'd left the front door open, Molly had no difficulty locating the quilts, both wrapped in clear plastic to protect them from dirt. She and little Sara were tugging on the top quilt, trying to move it inside.

"Here, let me do that," he said, touching her on the shoulder.

She jumped, as if she'd forgotten he was there.

Quinn was surprised at how much that thought bothered him. He wasn't used to being ignored. He stepped out on the porch and gathered the first quilt into his arms. Putting it on the rug that covered the entryway, he went back for the second one.

"Thank you so much for bringing them," Molly said, her voice breathless.

Quinn couldn't help thinking how that voice would affect him in a dark room, her body pressed close to his, the two of them alone. He cleared his throat. "Uh, you're welcome."

"Are we going to put them on the beds, Mommy?" Sara asked, her voice as enthusiastic as her mother's.

"Of course, sweetie," Molly said, but she didn't move.

Quinn wondered why she stood waiting. Then he realized she was waiting for him to leave, of course. He immediately started to make his departure, but his gaze fell on the wide graceful stairway that led to the second floor. How would Molly and delicate little Sara get those heavy quilts up the stairs?

"Let me carry the quilts upstairs for you," he said on impulse. After all, that was what Martha would want him to do.

"No, that's not necessary. You've already done so much, bringing them here. I didn't expect that," Molly assured him, her smile still bright.

"It won't take but a minute. Which one do you want first?"

"Are you sure?" she asked, the smile dimming as she searched his face.

He'd never worked so hard to do something for a lady in his life. "I'm sure. This one?"

The quilt he pointed to was the one the ladies had said was Bachelor's Puzzle. It had been done in various shades of blue.

"Yes, that would be great. I'll—I'll show you which room," she said, extending her hand to Sara.

The little girl, still excited, danced beside Molly as they started up the stairs.

So once again he followed Molly's entrancing backside up the stairs. And this time, as before, they were headed for a bed.

But not one they would share.

# Chapter Five

Molly had had long discussions about the colors for
each suite of rooms. The quilting ladies had promised
to select fabrics that would make the quilt the high-
light of each room. But today was the first time for
Molly to actually see if her plans were going to work
out.

She tried to look at the room with a stranger's eye.
Instead, she knew she was as coldly objective as a
grandmother beaming at her pride and joy.

As soon as Quinn put the quilt on the king-size
bed, she tore at the plastic, with Sara's help. Then
she spread the quilt over the bed, its edges stopping
after meeting the dark blue bed skirt.

"Perfect!" she exclaimed.

"The pillows, Mommy," Sara reminded her, running to the corner of the room where Molly had piled
up the pillows, waiting for the placement of the quilt.

"Oh, yes, Sara, thank you!" she exclaimed. She
joined her little girl in piling the pillows against the
brass headboard. Then the two of them stepped back,
hand in hand, and admired their handiwork.

"Very nice," a deep, masculine voice said, reminding Molly of their guest.

"Oh! I'm sorry, I didn't mean to keep you waiting. Thank you so much for carrying it up here."

"No problem. This room is beautiful. Did you use a decorator?"

"No!" She hadn't intended to answer so sharply, but the thought of turning her home over to some impersonal decorator was horrifying. "No, Sara and I planned everything. I had a little input from Jenna. She's an artist who—"

"I know Jenna," Quinn muttered. "She's my new sister-in-law."

"Oh. Yes, of course." She stood there awkwardly. "Where does the other quilt go?"

Molly wondered if she could ever appear at an advantage in front of this man. Today she was acting like a half-wit. Not that how she appeared to Quinn Spencer mattered, she sturdily assured herself. No, not at all.

"I'll show you," she said. The second quilt, A Young Man's Fancy, would go in the suite across the hall. She crossed to the door and opened it.

"I'll go get it," he said with a nod and started down the stairs.

He was being very helpful. More than she would've expected him to be. In fact, she felt quite guilty about thoughts she'd had of Quinn Spencer. He'd been helpful at every turn, from her legal difficulties to helping with Sara.

Today he was putting his muscles to use for her. And fine muscles they were, too. She couldn't help noticing his strong legs, his— Good heavens! She hadn't even asked him to take off his overcoat. Some hostess she was.

He carried the quilt into the other suite. Molly intended to wait to place the quilt until after she did a better job of welcoming and thanking the man. Sara, however, assumed they would spread the quilt out at once.

"Come on, Mommy!" she exclaimed, ripping the plastic away from the quilt.

"Here, I'll help," Quinn assured the little girl, a smile on his lips that only made him more attractive.

Before Molly could protest, the two of them had dispensed with the plastic covering. Then it seemed silly to protest spreading out the quilt. After all, it only took a moment. And she was anxious to see how it looked.

The three of them stood together and stared at the room. The greens of the quilt made the room appear fresh and inviting.

She couldn't stop herself from asking. "What do you think?"

"I think you've done a great job," he said, his voice soft and deep. A bedroom voice.

Stop that! Those thoughts were dangerous. She didn't want to connect this man with anything sexual. Intimate. Personal.

She drew a deep breath. "Thank you. You don't think either room is too...feminine?" She'd worried about that. After all, there was no male influence in their lives.

He turned to look at her, surprise on his face. "Not at all."

Her cheeks turned red. "Thanks. I haven't even asked you to take off your coat. I hope you haven't gotten overheated."

"No. And there's no need. I'm only going right back out, so—"

"Have you eaten lunch?" she asked, wondering where that impulse had come from. But she needed to thank him for his assistance.

"No," he answered, surprise on his face.

"I've got soup and salad ready for our lunch and there's plenty. I'd love to have you join us to say thank you."

Sara clapped her hands together. "Yes! Please, Mr. Man? And you could taste Mommy's muffins and vote, too."

"Sweetie, this is Mr. Spencer, not Mr. Man."

Sara beamed at Quinn, not at all bothered by having called him the wrong thing. "Please?"

QUINN OPENED HIS MOUTH to decline the invitation. But Sara's excitement stopped him. How could he disappoint her? It was flattering, too, that she was so excited at the idea that he would eat lunch with them.

"I don't want to put you to any trouble," he said in polite protest to Molly.

"No trouble at all. We usually eat in the kitchen, if you don't mind."

So she thought he was too proud to eat in a kitchen? "I like kitchens," he said. Not that he'd had a lot of experience with them, but what he'd seen of hers was inviting.

Sara took his hand and tugged toward the stairs. "Hurry! I'm hungry."

Her daughter's words shook Molly from her stiff formality. "How can you be that hungry? You tasted all the muffins!" she protested.

As Molly led the way down the stairs, Quinn asked, "What is this about muffins?"

"Oh, I was trying out my muffin recipes this

morning while Sara was at preschool. I had her taste them when she got home to see which one she liked best. I'm trying to decide which one to serve.''

''Ah, I'd be delighted to taste your muffins. What are my choices?'' Maybe they would help fill him up. Soup and salad didn't sound too substantial.

''Cranberry, orange spice, strawberry and banana nut,'' she returned as she moved down the stairs.

Sara, still holding his hand and hopping along beside him, said, ''I like the strawberry ones, but Mommy says she's 'fraid it tastes like cake.'' Sara beamed up at him. ''I like cake!''

The rueful look Molly sent him over her shoulder brought a chuckle, surprising him. Usually he didn't laugh all that often.

Once they reached the kitchen, she offered to take his overcoat. Shrugging out of it, he watched as she hung it on a coat tree standing near the back door.

''Taste test or lunch first?''

''Maybe I'd better test the muffins first before my taste buds get corrupted with lunch.''

''Sara, you set the table,'' Molly ordered. Then she gestured to the large kitchen table. ''Please, sit down. I'll bring the muffins to you. Would you like coffee or tea with them?''

''Coffee would be great.''

Sara importantly carried three place mats to the table and spread one out in front of Quinn. Then she returned to the cabinet where Molly had placed three plates and silverware. He'd almost protested when she'd ordered Sara to set the table. She was such a little thing, so young. He wasn't sure she was old enough to handle such a chore.

He was glad he'd kept quiet.

"You're doing a nice job, Sara," he praised.

"Thank you," she said, beaming at him again. "Mommy taught me."

"I bet you're a big help to Mommy," he replied. He'd never had many conversations with children and wasn't quite sure how to go about it.

"We're a team," Sara assured him.

"I can see that."

Molly set a cup of fragrant coffee in front of him, then returned to the cabinet for a plate. When she returned, he noted she'd cut some muffins into fourths. He looked up at her.

"I didn't think you'd want to eat four whole muffins, so I cut them up."

"Uh, thanks. Do I need to know which one is which?"

"No, it's probably better if you don't, in case you have any preconceived notions."

"About muffins?" he asked, a grin on his face. He'd never given muffins a moment's thought.

"Some people do. Like zucchini bread or carrot cake."

"Zucchini bread?" he asked, surprised.

"Yes. I thought about including it in the choices, but I wasn't sure—" She broke off abruptly. "I must be boring you to tears. It's bad enough that I'm subjecting you to tasting these." She set the plate down and returned to the kitchen area.

Sara leaned close, one little finger edging toward the plate of muffins. "This one is the strawberry one," she whispered.

"Sara!" Molly called sharply. "Let Mr. Spencer make his own choice."

A finger stole to the little girl's mouth and she looked sad. "Yes, Mommy."

"Did you put the napkins in place?" Molly continued.

Sara moved to do as her mother asked, but she kept her eye on Quinn.

To his amusement, he noted Molly did, too, only she tried to hide her interest. Sara didn't bother. This test tasting was serious business in the Blake household.

But not to him. He was going along with all this to be polite. That was all.

He took his first bite of muffin.

Hmm. Several distinct flavors lit up his taste buds.

Not bad. Not bad at all. He started to take a second bite of that muffin before he remembered he had three more to taste.

By the time he'd tasted all four muffins, he was ready to start again.

"You already tasted that one," Sara pointed out, now standing beside his chair in close observation.

Quinn shot Molly a look to see if she'd noticed. She had her back to him at the stove, stirring something. He leaned closer to Sara and whispered, "I need to taste them all again. I'm not sure yet."

"Oh. I tasted the strawberry one over and over again," Sara confessed.

Quinn wasn't slow. He knew a request when he heard one. He slid a bite of the strawberry muffin toward Sara. Quick as a wink, it disappeared.

Molly appeared beside the table, a tray in her hands. "Did you find one you liked?" she asked nonchalantly, as if his decision made no difference to her. But he'd seen her watching him. He knew differently.

He took a sip of coffee. "Well, actually—"

"You didn't like any of them," she guessed, disappointment in her voice. "I should've—"

"Molly," he interrupted, using her first name. You couldn't be formal over a kitchen table, he reasoned. "They're all terrific. I'm having trouble choosing between them."

"Really?" she asked, her face anxious.

The ridiculous idea of cupping her cheeks and kissing those luscious lips crossed his mind. He instantly dismissed it. "Uh, yeah, really. I taste one and think it's my favorite, until I taste the next one. Then it's my favorite. They're so moist."

"Thank you" was her only response. Then she set a big bowl in front of him.

He sniffed the steamy aroma arising from the bowl, but before he could identify it, she said, "Potato."

She added bowls for her and Sara, and several small bowls of condiments. "Bacon and cheese if you want any for your soup."

She returned to the cabinet to load three more bowls onto her tray. This time large salad bowls were placed on the table, along with several small pitchers of dressing. "The salad has chicken and cheese in it."

Then she put a glass of milk in front of Sara. "Would you like something else to drink, in addition to your coffee?" she asked him.

"Some ice water would be nice." He was beginning to think he was in a four-star restaurant. The soup smelled terrific. If it even came close to the perfection of the muffins, he was in for a treat.

Half an hour later, he wasn't sure he'd ever need to eat again. Not only had the food been wonderful, but also the company had pleased him. Sara had incredible table manners for a four-year-old. She also had a charm that entranced him. He laughed a couple of times as she entertained him with stories about the preschool she attended at the town's day care center.

Molly reminded her of her lunch occasionally.

Then Molly told her it was time for her afternoon "rest." It wasn't a nap, Sara assured him. She was too old for a nap. But Miss Kaitlin said they needed to rest so they'd grow taller. And she was going to grow this big, she told him, stretching her arm as high as she could reach.

After Molly returned from tucking Sara in for her "rest," she thanked him again for tasting the muffins.

He knew he could've easily excused himself at that point. She was giving him an opening. But he didn't take it.

"I can assure you, Molly, it was a pleasure. Anytime you need tasting done, I'm your man. You're an excellent cook."

She blushed and muttered another thank-you.

"Have you thought any about my suggestion?"

"Yes, I have. I'm planning an open house for a week from Sunday. But instead of having only the neighbors and a few dignitaries, I'm opening it to the entire town."

"The entire town?" he questioned, frowning. "Isn't that overdoing it just a little? It'll cost a lot."

"Not that much more. Everyone won't come, of

course, and I'm not serving a meal. Some muffins, some cake, snack food. It will give everyone a chance to look at the house. Of course, I'll only have the first two suites done because all the quilts aren't finished, but they'll be able to see what I'm trying to do.''

He couldn't imagine Molly and little Sara getting ready for such a huge undertaking. ''How will you manage?''

''Manage what?'' she asked, a frown on her face.

''All the work, the cleaning, the baking. I don't even know, but it sounds like a massive undertaking.''

''It won't be so bad. I've been talking to Eden about the flowers and—''

''You're going to have her do flower arrangements?'' he asked. The Garden of Eden, Eden Frazier's flower shop, was the most popular in town. ''Won't that be expensive?''

''No more than anyone else. We've worked out an arrangement where she delivers arrangements once a week for each suite, if it's being used.''

''Couldn't you use some fake arrangements? It would save money.''

She looked at him as if he'd suggested murder. ''Fake arrangements? No, never. Fresh flowers are so much better.''

''But you said money—''

She stiffened. ''Mr. Spencer, I told you I had my budget worked out. I'm not bankrupt.''

He caught himself before he could protest the use of his last name. It was a signal to back off. ''My apologies.''

But he made no move to leave.

After an awkward silence, she repeated, "Thank you for tasting the muffins."

"Why do you have to eliminate any of them? They're all wonderful."

"I thought I should have a signature muffin. You know, build a reputation for special things." She almost relaxed with her response until she appeared to remember that she was angry with him.

"I think you'll build a reputation for good food, whichever kind of muffin you serve. But variety might be fun. You could serve one kind each day of the week. You didn't have any blueberry muffins. Or surely there are other kinds." He searched his mind for kinds of muffins. He wasn't sure why he wanted the conversation to continue, but he did. "Maybe there are zucchini muffins?"

She smiled. "I could make pumpkin muffins."

"There you go! That would be perfect for Thanksgiving. Or turkey muffins, with the leftovers. Ham muffins for Easter. Rhubarb muffins."

She laughed at his silliness, and he grinned in return. Seeing Molly laugh was a delight in itself.

"You're being ridiculous."

"Maybe, but I think any kind of muffin you make would be good, if these are any indication."

"Sara was disappointed you didn't pick the strawberry one."

"I know," he agreed. "She kept pushing another bite toward me. Which was pretty impressive since she wanted to eat those bites herself."

"You noticed," Molly said with a grin. "I have to watch her. She has a definite sweet tooth."

"She's a beautiful little girl, both in her appearance and her behavior, Molly. You've done a great job raising her. Christopher would be proud.''

Suddenly the friendliness in the air, the warmth, the welcome, all disappeared. Molly's face was grim and closed. She stood. "Thank you for your help.''

"Wait!'' He hadn't intended the protest, but he wasn't going to be shoved out the door until he knew what he'd done wrong. "What did I do?''

She turned away, clearing the table. ''Nothing at all. I just don't want to take up more of your time. I know how busy you are.''

He stubbornly remained in his chair, as if standing would make it easier for her to dislodge him. ''It's Friday afternoon. I'm not so busy.''

"If you don't have work to do, I'm sure you have social plans. I don't want to make you run late.'' She kept her back to him, rinsing the dishes.

He decided to invade her space. Grabbing more dishes, he carried them to the sink. He couldn't have shocked her more if he'd slapped her.

"What are you doing?'' she demanded, outrage in her voice.

"Helping you.'' It seemed obvious to him, but not to her.

"I don't need your help!'' she assured him. "I can manage.''

"I can see that. Doesn't mean I shouldn't help, though. I do have manners, you know.''

"So, in a restaurant, you offer to clean the kitchen before you leave?''

"In a restaurant, I pay a bill, which covers cleaning the kitchen,'' he returned, keeping his voice level. He wanted to get to the bottom of what had upset her. So he wouldn't do it again. If she ever opened her door to him. Not that it mattered, of course, but there was no point in making enemies when it wasn't necessary.

"By the way," he added, before she could speak, "Amanda is coming back this evening. She'll be in the office on Monday."

"Good," she snapped, telling him without additional words she wouldn't be consulting him again.

He stood there, his hands on his hips, watching, trying to figure out how to scale the wall she'd built.

She turned and wiped her hands on a towel. "I'll get your coat for you."

"Wait just a minute," he protested. "I'm not going anywhere until you tell me what I said wrong."

# Chapter Six

Molly felt like an idiot.

The man had made a simple remark. If she'd contained her emotions, simply accepted his words for their good intentions, she wouldn't be in such an awkward position.

"You didn't say anything wrong, Mr. Spencer," she assured him quietly, keeping a tight rein on her emotions. "I overreacted."

"To what?"

"Your comment about Christopher." She headed toward the coatrack to get his overcoat. Surely her reasonableness would speed him on his way.

"But all I said was Christopher would be proud—"

"I know. As I said, a perfectly lovely sentiment." She held out the coat to him. He ignored it.

"I didn't realize your grief would still be so raw," he said, concern on his face, making her feel even worse.

The weight of the overcoat made it necessary to lower it against her body. "There is no grief."

She'd shocked him. He stared at her, saying nothing.

"I'm sorry. I know this is Christopher's hometown, and I've tried not to offend anyone. I'd appreciate it if you'd keep my remarks to yourself."

"But even if you and Christopher didn't— Sara was his daughter. Wasn't she?"

Molly stiffened. "Are you asking me if I was faithful to my husband?"

"No! No, I wouldn't— It's none of my business!"

"Sara is Christopher's daughter. But surely you don't find his attitude difficult to understand. I heard you explaining why you'd never have children."

Now he appeared as upset as her. Great. She'd turned a molehill into a mountain. Then she'd turned it into the Alps.

"My choices are irrelevant, Mrs. Blake. But surely, once Sara arrived—"

"Christopher ignored both of us. This is a pointless discussion, particularly after you've been so helpful." In a desperate attempt to make nice, she added, "Let me wrap up some of the muffins. You can have them for breakfast tomorrow."

She hurriedly put two of each type of muffin in a plastic bag and handed it to Quinn. Then she handed him his overcoat and led the way to the front door, praying he'd follow.

The sound of his heavy tread reassured her. She opened the front door and turned to face him. "Thank you again for your assistance."

"Thank you for a delicious lunch."

She nodded, anxious to have him on the other side of her closed door. Before she could make any more mistakes.

"Tell Sara goodbye for me."

That only made her feel even more guilty. He was

being very polite. "Of course. Thank you for your patience with her."

He nodded, but he didn't move.

She didn't know what else to say. Licking her suddenly dry lips, she ventured a look at him.

He smiled. "If we get any more polite, I'll have to bow before I leave."

Some of the tension left her shoulders. "I'm sorry. I don't seem to behave well around you, Mr. Spencer. But since Amanda is coming back to town, I shouldn't have to bother you again." There. That should satisfy him.

"I'll miss the muffins," he said with another smile.

She returned his smile, but she didn't make any offer to keep him supplied. Better to cut all ties.

Once again he told her goodbye and left the house.

She could finally shut him out of her life.

So why did she feel so empty?

QUINN DIDN'T RETURN to the office. He decided everything on his desk could wait until Monday. Instead, he went home.

He frowned. He was living with his father, in the family home. When he'd come back to Tyler, he'd been like a bird with a broken wing. He'd needed to heal. Having finally gotten his courage to risk his heart, he'd found it tossed back into his lap, rejected. Marietta, the woman he'd thought he loved, had had a bigger target. She'd met an Englishman with a title.

While he'd told himself it was his pride, more than anything, that had been hurt, he'd found himself reliving the rejection he'd felt in his childhood, when his mother had disappeared from his life.

And he'd vowed never again to risk his heart.

It took too much energy to care about where he lived, so he'd returned to his old bedroom. But now, after time spent at Molly's, his choice seemed so…so sterile. The housekeeper his father hired, Eva, kept everything clean. But there was none of the warmth, the pride, the caring, that was obvious in Molly's house.

None of the smiles.

He thought of Sara's infectious laughter, her beaming smile. Those big blue eyes that could look so guilty for the smallest infraction.

He'd never realized how much a child could play on one's emotions. How easily she could worm her way into a man's heart. How protective he felt.

What kind of idiot had Christopher been? Maybe it would take time to warm up to having a child. But Molly? He had ignored Molly?

Sara's brightness and warmth came directly from Molly. A man would never be cold in a household with those two. And at night, his mind immediately continued, picturing one of the king-size beds, he'd be in heaven.

He immediately dismissed that thought. She was a mother, damn it. He shouldn't be thinking of her as a—as a woman. A sexy woman.

But he couldn't seem to help himself.

That night, his dreams were warm, happy ones, centered around two blondes. When he awoke the next morning, he was reluctant to leave his bed, knowing it would dispel the lingering remnants of his dreams.

Yesterday afternoon he'd placed the muffins in the refrigerator. This morning he hurried to the kitchen and heated them in the microwave, eager to again taste Molly's handiwork.

"Something smells good," Elias growled as he came into the kitchen just as the muffins came out of the microwave.

Quinn jerked in a guilty start. "Uh, yeah. Muffins."

"Ah. You went to the bakery."

He didn't lie. But he didn't correct his father's guess, either. What difference did it make?

His father selected one of the muffins. Quinn noted that he'd chosen one of the strawberry ones. He grinned. His father had a sweet tooth, too, like Sara.

After pouring two cups of coffee, he carried them to the table and slid one to his father, who'd just taken his first bite.

"Hey, this is good," Elias intoned. "What kind—"

"Strawberry."

"Never tasted anything like it before. Are they all strawberry?"

"No." He named the other kinds, watching his father survey the plate. He could tell he wouldn't have any muffins left over.

He was sure of that when the back door opened and Brady came in. He almost groaned.

"I brought some doughnuts," Brady announced before he saw the muffins. "What's this? Has Quinn become Betty Crocker overnight?"

Quinn didn't respond and Elias was too interested in what he was eating. "Taste this," he ordered his second son, pinching off a piece of his muffin.

While Brady and his father discussed the strawberry muffin, Quinn took a knife and cut the remaining muffins in half. He wanted some of each of them and he was going to have to share.

Fortunately, there weren't any questions. The men were concentrating on the taste, with muttered appreciation when they tasted a new one.

Until there was nothing but crumbs on the plate.

"I think we may have to buy stock in the bakery," Elias commented as he sipped his coffee.

Brady protested, "But that's where I bought those doughnuts. I didn't see anything like these." He waved at the empty plate. "I don't think they came from the bakery."

"But Quinn said—"

"No, I didn't. You guessed the bakery and I didn't correct you."

"So are you telling me you made them? Do I have a son who intends to give up law to be a baker now?"

Quinn shook his head. "A friend made them." He'd hoped to avoid any more questions, but his father perked up like a retired fire horse put between the traces for one last run.

"I didn't know you had any friends who could cook. I thought they all dined in restaurants."

Brady snapped his fingers. "It's the blonde. She wanted to say thank-you for taking her little girl to the hospital. Why didn't she send me some muffins? I'm the one who made her well."

Quinn sipped his coffee and avoided looking at his relatives.

"A looker and she can cook like this? I think I want to meet this lady," Elias said.

"You'll have your chance. She's having an open house for the entire town next weekend," he said, determined to keep everything impersonal. "She owns the new bed-and-breakfast in town, on Ivy Lane."

"The old Blake house?" Brady asked. "I heard something about that, but I hadn't made the connection to Molly. Interesting. Did she buy it?"

"She inherited it. She's Christopher's widow." Quinn remembered their last conversation. Not a grieving widow, she'd told him. He was surprised at how much relief that thought gave him.

"Christopher Blake was no prize," Elias said.

"I don't remember much about him," Brady said. "What was wrong with him?"

Quinn waited for his father's answer with great curiosity. He remembered the man vaguely, but they'd never been friends.

"He was a pretentious snob, interested only in himself. He neglected his mother shamelessly." Elias didn't forgive a lack of family consideration.

Molly had said Christopher ignored her and Sara. An even greater sin than ignoring his mother, in Quinn's eyes.

"What's the blonde like?" Elias asked.

Quinn considered his answer. He didn't want to sound too enthusiastic, because his father would read more into it than he intended. But he had to be honest. "She's a ray of sunshine. She and Sara. And a hard worker. Wait until you see the house. She's done wonders with it."

"Hasn't Jenna been working with her? Seems to me I've heard her mention something about a bed-and-breakfast." Brady stared at Quinn, waiting for his answer.

He nodded.

"I believe I'll plan on going to that open house. When did you say it would be?" Elias asked.

"Next Sunday afternoon."

"You going?" Brady asked.

Quinn realized both men were watching for his response. Damn. He hadn't been able to throw them off the trail. "I guess so," he said, trying for an offhand manner. "After all, she's our client."

"Ah," Elias said. "Maybe we can all go together, so you can introduce us. I'd like to thank her for the muffins."

WHAT A HECTIC WEEK!

In addition to the open house on Sunday, Sara's birthday fell on Friday. Four days a week, Sara was at the preschool program at Kaity's Kids day care until three-thirty. On Friday, though the day care center remained open, the preschool ended at noon. It was the perfect time for Sara's birthday party, so Molly was hosting twelve four-year-olds for the afternoon.

Kaitlin Rodier, the owner of the day care, was coming, of course. Her workers would take care of the other age groups at the center. But Sara had insisted her teacher be invited.

Since Kaitlin was one of Molly's closest friends, she was delighted to have her come, but she was also afraid it would seem like work to Kaitlin. After all, she would've already spent the morning with the small guests.

But Molly could use the help.

Since she was inviting the entire town to the open house, she'd decided the best way would be to put an invitation in the paper on Friday, Saturday and

Sunday. Jenna had promised to take care of that chore, and she stopped by on Wednesday morning with the ad to show her.

"Oh, Jenna, that's wonderful!" Molly enthused. The large square had the rose and tulip entwined with ivy. "And they'll be able to print it in color?"

"Yeah. It's going to look terrific."

"Yes, it will. Eden is going to do some flower arrangements that will reflect our logo."

"She does very good work. I've been in there several times," Jenna agreed.

"And how are you feeling? You're not doing too much, are you?" Molly asked. Jenna had recently married, but she was already pregnant. The entire town had been talking about her and Quinn's older brother Seth.

"I'm fine. Seth won't let me do too much. And his family…if I even hint at wanting something, they all jump up at once. A woman could get used to this."

Molly blinked several times. "Even Quinn? I thought he wasn't interested in children."

"I don't know about that, but he's been very nice to me." Jenna looked at Molly. "Didn't I hear he was doing some work for you?"

"Um, he helped out while Amanda was out of town."

"Ah. Well, I've got to run, but if there's anything else you need done, just let me know. I should be picking up your order for stationery next week."

"Great. I appreciate all the work."

"I appreciate the business," Jenna replied with a smile.

After Jenna left, Molly vacuumed the rug in the

entryway, polished the banister on the stairway and swept the hardwood floors.

Then she broke for lunch. While she ate, she made her shopping list for Sara's party. She'd received specific instructions from her child about what to serve. Frankly, hot dogs didn't enchant Molly. Nor could she demonstrate her cooking skills with such mundane fare.

But the party wasn't about her. It was for Sara, and she'd requested hot dogs.

Then Molly made a second shopping list for the weekend. She planned to have the house spotless by Friday evening. If she kept the party contained to the kitchen and breakfast area, that shouldn't be too difficult.

Saturday she'd do all the cooking, except for the last-minute preparations. Sunday she'd be relaxed and ready to greet her neighbors.

After lunch, she continued to polish and scrub. Sara would be brought by the car pool she and several other mothers had organized. Tuesdays and Fridays were her days to drive, so today she could remain at home.

At three-fifteen the doorbell rang. Checking her watch, she wondered if school had let out early. Hurrying to the door, she swung it open, her gaze fixed on where Sara's head would be.

Then traveled up the dark overcoat until it reached Quinn's face. She hadn't seen him since their embarrassing encounter last Friday.

And she had no idea why he was here now.

She'd discussed her case with Amanda by phone. Amanda assured her Quinn had handled everything.

"What— I mean, hello, Mr. Spencer."

"Hello, Molly."

When he stood there, saying nothing else, she asked, "Did you want to come in?" She couldn't imagine why, but politeness demanded that she offer.

With a smile he went past her, already removing his overcoat. He planned to stay?

"I hope you don't mind," he said with a smile. "I was in the neighborhood and I thought I'd check on arrangements for Sunday. I feel sort of responsible since it was my idea."

She stared at him. "But you offered it as a suggestion. It was my decision to go ahead with it," she assured him, frowning. "You have no reason to feel responsible."

He shrugged. "Maybe not. But I hear a lot of people are coming. I thought I should warn you you might have a crowd."

"But I haven't even advertised it yet. How could you hear—"

He chuckled, almost a rusty tone, as if he didn't often laugh. It was an entrancing sound. "This is a small town. I certainly mentioned it to my father. It seems he's visiting with Lydia a lot. He discussed it with her. She, of course, told the ladies at Worthington House, who in turn told—"

"I get the picture." Molly nodded. "Well, I appreciate your letting me know."

After a pause, he said, "I wouldn't turn down a cup of coffee, if you have any made. It's been a long day."

Molly was horrified by her lapse in good manners. The man threw her off track every time. "Of course. Do you mind the kitchen?"

"I love your kitchen," he assured her with a smile.

"You don't happen to need any muffins tasted, do you?"

She couldn't hold back a return smile. "No, but you could test the oatmeal-raisin cookies. I put pecans in the recipe this time."

"I'll sacrifice myself for the good of science," he agreed with a heavy sigh and a grin that signaled his playacting.

"How big of you," she agreed solemnly, and led the way to the kitchen.

"It probably will be," he said, following her. "I'll probably put on unwanted pounds with all this testing."

With a quick look over her shoulder, she muttered, "I don't think you're in any danger." In fact, he looked just about perfect from her point of view. Not that she was interested, of course. She'd looked for the sake of science.

Seated at the table with a steaming cup of coffee and a plate of cookies in front of him, Quinn asked, "Aren't you going to join me?"

She poured herself a cup of coffee and sat down across from him. "I'll let you do the tasting, since I've already tried a few too many."

He bit into the first cookie and closed his eyes to savor the taste. Then he finished that one and reached for another. "I'd better try more than one. For quality control, you know. That one could be a rogue cookie that didn't conform to the rest of them."

"True," she agreed, and nudged the plate closer to him.

"So how are plans shaping up for Sunday?"

"I'm pretty much on schedule. Oh, here's the ad that will be in the paper. I've decided to run it Friday,

Saturday and Sunday, so everyone will see it.'' She proudly displayed the paper Jenna had brought by earlier. ''Jenna—I mean your sister-in-law—did it for me.''

''Very nice.''

''Yes, she's been a real godsend. I wasn't sure I'd be able to find what I needed in such a small town, but she's designed my stationery, my invoices, my business cards, everything I'll need. And once I finalize my menus, she'll do those, too.''

''Are you serving anything but breakfast?''

''Not really. But I figured offering a late-night snack, like a pot of coffee and cookies or something like that, might be a good idea. And on Sundays, maybe a brunch that would be open to the public, too.''

''That's pretty ambitious,'' he said, a frown on his face.

Molly felt herself stiffen and drew a deep breath. ''I'm an ambitious person. I want my business to succeed.''

He reached for another cookie. ''I don't see how it could fail. And if it does, you can open a bakery. We don't really have a first-class bakery in town.''

About to answer him, Molly froze. Why hadn't she thought of that? Friday, when she made Sara's birthday cake, she could show off her skills. And the Christmas cake she intended to make for her open house. If she printed up a notice about special occasion baking, she might be able to generate more income. And she loved baking.

''Molly? Molly, did I say something wrong?''

She beamed at him. ''No! You've given me another idea! I can offer special occasion baking to order. After all, I'll have my afternoons free even after I open. I could use that time to— I'll call Jenna and get her to make me a sign for Sunday that discreetly advertises my services. What a wonderful idea!''

''I didn't mean you should do more work. You've already taken on a big job, Molly. I'm not sure—''

The sound of a car horn interrupted his warning.

''Sara's home! I'll be right back.'' She hurried to the front door. When she came back in with Sara, Quinn still sat at the table. Somehow, she'd expected him to disappear.

Having prepared Sara, she was gratified when her child greeted Quinn properly. ''Hi, Mr. Spencer. You came to see us!''

Quinn returned her daughter's big smile. ''Yes, I did. How are you?''

Suddenly Molly knew what was coming, but she didn't see any way to avoid it. She didn't want this man involved in her life. He was too much of a temptation. Both to her and Sara. And she was sure he wasn't interested.

But Sara, a beaming smile on her face, was about to make it difficult to keep him away.

# Chapter Seven

"I'm having a birthday in two days," Sara exclaimed. "Will you come to my party?"

Quinn stared at the little girl. She was as bright and charming as he'd remembered. Just like her mother. "Your party? You're having a party for your birthday?"

"Yes. On Friday. And we're having hot dogs!" Sara announced, obviously considering the menu to be the pièce de résistance.

"No!" Molly began.

"I'd love to," Quinn said at the same time. How could he turn Sara down?

"Mr. Spencer, you're not thinking. Sara, Mr. Spencer will have to be at work. He can't come to the party."

"But he said yes, Mommy. Didn't you, Mr. Spencer?"

"Yes, I did. What time is your party?" Molly's obvious reluctance to have him come to Sara's party only made it more important for him to be there.

"When we come home from school," Sara informed him.

He looked at his watch. "Of course I can leave work a little early."

"On Fridays, school lets out at noon. And there will be twelve four-year-olds, Mr. Spencer. I don't think you want to be a part of that." Molly kept her voice low, as if hoping her daughter wouldn't realize she was discouraging him.

"I'll get presents and everything. I've never had a party before!" The excitement built in Sara's voice.

"I can't wait," Quinn assured her with a wink. He thought about his own childhood. There had been only a couple of birthday parties, where his father took him and several friends to a pizza place for a brief marking of his special day. He was pleased that Sara would have a real celebration.

And he was surprised at how much he wanted to be a part of it. If the decision had been left to Molly, he knew he wouldn't be invited. But she loved her child too much to deny her invitation to Quinn.

Molly poured a glass of milk for Sara and got her her own saucer of cookies. Then she put her at a small table in front of a portable television over near the window. "It's time for *Sesame Street,* sweetie."

"Okay. Do you like Cookie Monster?" she asked Quinn before she sat down.

"Uh, yeah," he assured her with a smile.

Beside him, Molly muttered, "You have no idea who that is, do you?"

"Not a clue," he whispered. "Is he bad or good?"

She shook her head in despair. "When you get back to the office, call and tell me you've got to see a client on Friday afternoon. I'll explain to Sara."

It took him a minute to realize she was giving him

a way out from attending the party. "Are you taking back my invitation?"

She plopped down onto the chair next to him, a disgusted look on her face. "Quinn Spencer, I'm trying to give you an out to make up for your monumentally bad decision to accept Sara's invitation."

"Bad for me, or bad for you?"

Stunned, she stared at him. "Bad for me? Why would your coming to Sara's party be bad for me?"

"I have no idea, but you sure are working hard to discourage me."

"Didn't you hear me? There will be twelve four-year-olds, all eating sugar. You'll hate it."

"How do you know?"

"You hate kids! I heard you!"

He was growing tired of the conversation she'd overheard being used to condemn him. "I did not say I hated kids. I said I didn't have room for them in my life."

"Well, there you go. Obviously, Friday will be inconvenient for you."

"But I hadn't met Sara," he added, as if she hadn't spoken. "She's—she's special. And I want to come to her birthday party."

"Fine," she snapped. "Put on something wash-and-wear and take two aspirin before you come. And don't say I didn't warn you!"

AFTER MOLLY'S CHALLENGE, Quinn was prepared to show her he could handle something as innocuous as a child's birthday party.

And he was sure he could. The big difficulty wouldn't be the party, but what present to buy. After discarding a lot of different ideas, on Thursday he took his problem to the one group of people on whom he could always rely.

The Quilting Circle.

"Sara's having a birthday party?" Martha exclaimed. "I bet my great-grandson, Jeremy, will be there. He and Sara are best friends, don't you know."

"No, I didn't know," Quinn said. "Would you like to go to the party with me? I'm sure Molly wouldn't mind."

Martha's face lit up. "Me? I'd love to— Oh, no, it'd be too much trouble for you."

"Not at all. In fact," he said, leaning closer, "I need a friend. Molly didn't think I should come. Is it that bad? I never— I mean I haven't attended a children's party in years."

"Of course not. They're just noisy. Can't keep little kids in their chairs," Martha told him.

"Then I'll pick you up at noon on Friday. And we're having hot dogs. Sara seems to think it'll be a prime treat."

"Wonderful."

"Now, here's my real problem. What do I get her for a present?"

Martha and Quinn, along with some input from the others, discussed the perfect gift for at least half an hour. Then, promising to find a gift for Martha, too, and get it wrapped, he headed for Gates Department Store.

That evening, with his purchases sitting proudly wrapped in the den, he called Molly.

It was eight o'clock, after Sara's bedtime, so he expected to have Molly's full attention.

Instead, she answered the phone as she always

seemed to do when he talked with her. Breathless. "Hello?"

"Is everything all right?"

"Quinn? Um, yes, well, just a minute."

He sat in silence, straining to hear what was going on. It relieved him that he could hear no voices, particularly male voices, in the background.

Finally she returned to the phone. "I'm sorry. I—"

"Do you need help? Should I come over?"

"Come over? Help with what?"

"I don't know," he growled. "You sounded like something was wrong." He didn't like not knowing what was happening to Molly.

"No, I had Sara's cake in the oven and it needed to come out. I couldn't let it burn, that's all."

He noticed that she seemed less breathless now. More in control. "Okay, sorry, bad timing."

"That's all right. Are you calling to tell me you can't make it tomorrow?"

She sounded pleased. Did she want him to stay away that badly? Well, too bad. He wasn't disappointing Sara. "No. I'm calling to ask if I can bring a date."

"A date?"

She sounded shocked. Did she think he couldn't get a date if he wanted one? Or maybe, just maybe, she didn't like the idea of him with another woman. That thought pleased him a lot more than her not wanting him in her house did.

"Yeah. I was talking to Martha about the party and she said her great-grandson would be there."

"Yes, of course, but—but what does that have to do with you bringing a date?"

She still sounded upset.

He chuckled. "Martha. I asked her if she wanted to come."

He waited as she remained silent.

Finally she said, "You're asking if you can bring Martha to Sara's party?"

"Yes."

"And a date?"

His smile grew wider. "I meant Martha would be my date."

"Oh. We'd be delighted to have Martha come to the party." She cleared her throat. "Are you still coming?"

"Of course I'm coming. I'm bringing Martha. And we're both counting on hot dogs."

"I'll be sure to buy extras," she said, a touch of something he couldn't recognize in her voice. "But there will also be chicken casserole and salad if you'd prefer."

"Perfect," he murmured, and was sure it would be. "Anything I can do to help?"

"When you get here, you can unload the little tables and chairs Kaitlin is loaning me."

"Martha and I will get there early, about noon. I'm looking forward to it. Is Sara excited?"

Molly groaned and Quinn's stomach clenched. "Oh, yes. It's all she can talk about."

"And you?"

"And me, what?"

"Is everything okay with you? Everything still on track for Sunday?"

"Yes. This afternoon, the columnist for the 'Life-styles' section at the paper, Gina Santori, called and came over to interview me about the bed-and-breakfast. I thought that was a good thing, don't you?''

"Yeah, I do. Gina will do a nice job writing you up. Did she like everything?"

"Oh, yes. I made some more muffins, the strawberry ones, to serve her. She wanted the recipe."

"I'm not surprised. Everyone reads her column. That will be great advertising. Did she see the bedrooms?"

"Yes. Sara led the tour," she added.

He chuckled. "I bet she helped eat the muffins, too."

"You know she did," Molly agreed with a laugh that sent shivers through Quinn. He wished he could see her smile.

"Did Gina say she'd come Sunday?"

"Yes, she did, and she's going to bring a photographer and do a complete article for the paper to run after Christmas, which will help me fill up for the inn's opening in February, for Valentine's day weekend. I want my place to be the first thing to come to mind when someone is planning a romantic getaway. A place where lovers meet."

Quinn couldn't speak for a moment, images of lovers under the quilts. When he realized he was picturing himself and Molly, he hurriedly cleared his throat and said, "Wow, you must've charmed the socks off her," he said, teasing, but he knew he was right. Gina had discriminating taste; he wasn't surprised she was won over by Molly and Sara.

Molly laughed again. "I doubt that, but she was very nice. I'll enjoy reading her column even more now that I've met her."

Quinn was pleased for Molly. "Anything I need to bring for tomorrow?"

"Oh, no, if you'll help Kaitlin unload when you get here, that will be more than enough."

"Then I'll see you tomorrow. I'm looking forward to it," he finished with his voice husky, thinking of being in Molly's presence again tomorrow.

After he'd hung up the phone, he sat with his hand on it, picturing Molly in her kitchen, a big apron wrapped around her trim figure, her cheeks flushed with heat, the house smelling like heaven.

He'd vowed to stay away from her, of course, and he intended to. But not at Sara's expense. It wouldn't hurt to celebrate the little sprite's birthday. Birthdays should be special.

And Sara had a mother who knew how to make each day one of a kind. She was a lucky little girl.

MOLLY STARED AT HERSELF in the mirror. She was getting better at duplicating the style the hairdresser had given her. She decided she looked her best this morning.

Not that her appearance mattered, she hurriedly assured herself. After all, it was Sara's party, not hers.

She hurried out of her bedroom and down two flights of stairs before she had to admit that she'd worried over her appearance because of Quinn's attendance at the party. Assuming he actually showed up.

If Christopher were the one Sara expected, Molly would've already started preparing her daughter for her father's nonappearance. The way things turned out, she supposed she should be grateful Christopher had spent so little time with Sara. When he died, Sara had only been two. Now she scarcely remembered the man who was her father.

And after today, she felt sure Quinn would disappear as well. She just hoped Sara wouldn't be hurt. Maybe the excitement of the day would de-emphasize Quinn's attendance. Sara would be pleased that Martha would be there. She liked the elderly lady. Though that could be because of the candy Martha always had on hand.

Molly was almost to the kitchen when a knock on the front door stopped her. She checked her watch. It was twenty until twelve. Had Quinn come even earlier than he'd said?

Her heart sped up as she hurried to the door. Bundled up against the cold, Martha beamed at her. But no smile could outshine Quinn's as he stood behind the elderly woman.

"Are we too early?" he asked.

"Not at all. Come on in before you freeze to death."

She took Martha's arm and led her into the house, then helped her out of her coat and scarf. "We're having the party in the kitchen. If you'll come on back, I'll fix you something hot to drink."

"I'm going back out to get the presents," Quinn said as she and Martha started toward the kitchen.

"Oh, you shouldn't have—"

Quinn looked offended. "Of course we should have. It's Sara's birthday." He left without waiting for her response.

"But it's enough that you both came. Sara is so excited about you being here," she told Martha.

"Don't spoil the boy's fun," Martha returned.

"He didn't have a very happy childhood. I think he's as excited as Sara."

Martha's words were tucked away to be examined later. "I doubt it. Sara could scarcely eat breakfast."

They entered the kitchen.

"My, this is such a big, lovely room," Martha said. "A perfect room for a family."

Molly surveyed the room through Martha's eyes. The dining area attached to the kitchen was large. She'd made it into a small family room with the television and some chairs, a comfy couch. She and Sara spent a lot of their time there.

"Thank you. I work in here a lot and Sara stays here with me."

"You're a good mother," Martha said as she patted her arm.

"Where are we putting the presents?" Quinn asked as he walked into the kitchen.

Molly stared at the big box he carried, a smaller box sitting on top of it. "What did you buy? You didn't spend too much money, did you? A small gift should—"

"I bought something I thought Sara would like," he assured her, frowning.

Martha squeezed her arm slightly and smiled, barely shaking her head. Molly remembered Martha's earlier words and changed the subject. "Is coffee okay, Martha? Or I can make hot tea."

"Coffee would be wonderful. You want some, Quinn?"

"Sure do. Molly's coffee is great." He put the presents on the floor against the wall and slipped out of his overcoat, hanging it on the coatrack by the back door. As if he visited all the time.

She hastily poured coffee, not wanting to think about Quinn as a regular visitor. It brought too many headaches.

"No strawberry muffins?" he asked as he sat down.

"No, I'm not serving muffins today."

"Strawberry muffins?" Martha asked, her gaze darting back and forth between the two of them.

"I took a muffin-tasting test for Molly. She makes great muffins," Quinn explained. "I even took some home. Dad and Brady loved them, too."

Molly stared at Quinn's appearance, finally noticing he wasn't in a suit, as he'd always been in the past. He'd taken her at her word and dressed in jeans and a flannel shirt. He looked so rugged and charming, she regretted her advice. The casual clothes made him much too approachable. Not a good thing.

The sound of a car in the driveway distracted her. "I think Kaitlin is here." She hurried to the back door, only to discover Quinn on her heels.

"Will she have the children with her?"

"Some of them. Jeremy's mother is helping, too. Pam Kelsey. She's a coach at the high school." She took a deep breath, feeling that she was babbling.

"I know Pam," Quinn assured her. "I grew up here, remember?" He grabbed his coat and stepped outside. Then he looked at her. "Where's your coat?"

"I'm just going to be out here a minute." Her new cream sweater and navy wool pants would keep her warm enough to get the kids inside.

Like ants scurrying toward a crumb, children poured from the two vehicles, headed straight for them.

"This way, children. Sara, don't run. Hurry in so you won't get cold," Molly called, enjoying seeing her daughter with her friends. Since their arrival in Tyler, Sara had had the opportunity to learn to play with others. Molly was pleased with her child's progress.

"Mommy, Mommy!" Sara called. "I want to show everyone my bedroom. Can I? Can I take them upstairs?"

That would give Quinn time to get the small tables inside and set up. "Yes, if you'll be careful on the stairs. Don't go too fast for everyone." She'd lectured her daughter on her responsibilities as hostess.

Like a whirlwind blowing through the kitchen, twelve little children hurried across the room, pausing only for Jeremy and Sara to greet Martha.

Molly remained at the back door, greeting Pam as she reached the kitchen, and holding the door wide for both Quinn and Kaitlin. Then she went out to Kaitlin's van to gather some of the plastic chairs. Quinn returned for the last table and some of the chairs.

"I can get them, Molly. You don't have a coat on," he reminded her.

"So I'll go back inside with some chairs," she returned mildly. She should protest his attempt to protect her, but it was so sweet, she couldn't bring herself to do so. Of course, it meant nothing, but, still, it felt good.

Once everything was unloaded, they returned to the warmth of the kitchen.

After putting down the chairs, Molly hurried over to pour more coffee.

"Where are the kids?" Quinn asked, a puzzled look on his face.

"Sara wanted to show her friends her bedroom," Molly explained. Suddenly Quinn was at her side, taking the coffee she'd poured for Pam and Kaitlin and carrying it to the table.

Molly saw the look the three women exchanged and grew flustered. She poured Quinn's cup of coffee as he returned to her side.

"Aren't you having any?" he asked.

"Not right now. I want to get the hot dogs on the tables before the kids come back down. They're always starved after school."

"We'll help," Pam said, starting to get up.

Before Molly could speak, Quinn said, "Sit down, Pam. I'll help Molly. I haven't been working all morning, like you have." He added, "You, too, Kaitlin. Martha's been looking forward to visiting with you."

"She sees me when I come to the Quilting Circle," Kaitlin protested with a smile for Martha.

Since Quinn seemed insistent on helping, Molly had him pour milk into twelve small party cups and put them at each place setting, while she put the boiled wieners on buns and placed them on party plates. She already had several kinds of chips in bowls.

She'd prepared two trays with condiments on them. She'd intended to ask Kaitlin to start at one end of the long table while she began at the other, helping each child personalize his or her hot dog. But Quinn seemed to figure out what she needed before she said anything and took one of the trays just as the children came racing back into the kitchen.

"We're hungry!" Sara announced, excitement in her voice.

"Lunch is ready. Everyone sit down," Molly directed.

"Now I know how the cowboys felt when the herd stampeded," Quinn murmured as he passed by her.

"And they haven't had sugar yet," she warned him, but she couldn't help smiling.

As soon as the children began eating, the noise level descended. Molly hurried to the stove to take out a dish of her chicken casserole. Quinn took it from her and carried it to the table. She fetched the salad, ready except for the dressing, from the refrigerator. The rolls were in the lower oven, ready to eat.

In no time, everyone was served.

"My, Quinn, I had no idea you were so handy around the kitchen," Martha teased.

Molly expected Quinn to protest. Instead, he laughed at Martha. "It's not hard to be helpful when all you have to do is put the food on the table. The skill is in making it. Like this chicken casserole. It's terrific, Molly."

She muttered a thank-you, her cheeks aflame. Christopher had never expressed any appreciation for her cooking, much less offered to help.

"In fact, I only see one thing Molly's failed at," Quinn added, a grin on his face.

She should've known. He was too good to be true. Christopher had frequently listed her faults in front of guests. It seemed Quinn intended to do the same.

Holding her breath, she steeled herself for his criticism.

# Chapter Eight

It hadn't occurred to Quinn that anyone would take his words seriously. How could they? Molly was so incredibly talented. Combining her skills with the love she put into her work, she was unparalleled as a mother and homemaker.

But the look on her face told him he'd made a mistake. Keeping his smile in place, he explained, "She didn't teach Sara that her chicken casserole is much better than a hot dog."

The other ladies laughed. Molly stared at him, a look of disbelief on her face.

Had her husband not appreciated her? Had Christopher been cruel to her? That thought had Quinn's stomach clenching in anger and disgust.

"We're ready for birthday cake!" Sara announced in a loud voice, followed by cheers from the other children.

Molly wrenched her gaze from him and left her unfinished meal to tend to the children. He immediately followed her.

"Can I help?"

"No, I'll manage, thank you. Go finish your casserole."

"My turn to help," Pam said behind him, having followed them. "Go keep Martha company. I know you're a favorite of hers."

But Quinn didn't want to be dismissed. As Molly began clearing away the paper plates with the remains of the hot dogs, he grabbed a trash bag and held it open for her as she rounded the table.

"Thank you, but it's not necessary."

"It'll be faster."

He felt someone tugging on his shirt and discovered Sara behind him.

"Mr. Spencer, have you seen my cake?"

"No, Sara, I haven't. Is it chocolate?"

"Yes, and it's Mickey!" Sara's face was beaming.

"Mickey?" he asked, not quite sure of the significance of her words.

"Mickey Mouse!" Sara clarified. "Mommy made it!"

"I want to see!" Jeremy called, followed by the other children, jumping out of their chairs to follow Sara.

"Back in your seats, so we can bring the cake to the table," Molly calmly ordered. "If you're not in your chair, I won't be able to give you any cake and ice cream."

There was a concerted rush to the chairs. Several tumbled over, and Quinn abandoned the trash bag to restore order.

Molly crossed to the kitchen and opened a cabinet, bringing out a large plate holding a cake in the shape of Mickey Mouse's head. The children oohed and aahed when they saw the cake. The ladies came over to surround the little tables as Molly inserted candles into the icing.

"Did you do the cake yourself?" Pam asked.

"Yes," Molly answered as she lit the candles.

Quinn was amazed. He'd occasionally seen decorated cakes in a bakery, but they hadn't looked any better than Molly's.

She led the little group in a round of "Happy Birthday," then ordered the delighted Sara to make a wish and blow out the candles. When that ritual had been performed, amid lots of cheers, the dishing out of cake and ice cream began.

When all the children had been served, Quinn returned to his chicken casserole, promising Sara he'd eat some of her cake later. He was discovering that small children rushed through everything at a birthday party. If he'd tried to eat that fast, he'd have indigestion.

He noticed Molly barely ate anything. She was too busy supervising the children and moving on to the next stage before they could get impatient.

"She's good, isn't she?" Martha whispered as Molly returned to the children's table to settle a dispute.

"Absolutely," Kaitlin agreed. "I'd love to have her come work for me, but she's too busy. I hope the bed-and-breakfast succeeds."

"It has to," Quinn said. "She's too good. Once anyone eats her cooking, or sees how much effort she's put into the house, they won't be able to resist."

"I think we need to find her a husband, though," Martha said quietly.

Quinn tried to hide the sudden protest that welled up in him. "I'm not sure she's interested in a husband."

"Probably not after being married to Christopher," Martha said crisply. "But Sara needs a father, and Molly could use some help around here."

"She's managing just fine," he insisted. The thought of Molly and another man didn't seem right to him, but he didn't examine his feelings too closely.

"Are you coming to the open house on Sunday?" Kaitlin asked him, changing the subject.

"Yeah, of course. I think Dad and Brady are coming, too. And I'm sure Seth and Jenna will be here. Jenna has designed Molly's stationery and things."

"From what I hear," Pam inserted, "I think most of the town will be here. There's a lot of curiosity, partly caused by Ursula's animosity."

"That woman is half-crazy, don't you know," Martha said.

Quinn realized it was Ursula's behavior that had sent Molly running to his office. Not such a bad thing.

"It's time to open presents!" Sara announced.

"Sara," Molly remonstrated quietly, "your friends haven't finished their cake and ice cream yet."

"Hurry!" Sara exclaimed.

Quinn suspected Sara's response wasn't quite what Molly had hoped for.

Kaitlin rose from the table. "I think it's time for cleanup again."

Martha started to get up. Quinn reached out a hand and stopped her. "You stay put, Martha. I'll help."

Martha nodded.

As he moved away from the table, he heard Pam

murmur, "My, I had no idea Quinn was so—so do-mesticated."

Truth to tell, he hadn't, either. If someone had told him a month ago that he'd be attending a child's birthday party, he'd have laughed in his face. But it seemed so right to be at Sara's party.

To be helping Molly.

Being part of the afternoon's events satisfied something he hadn't even known he needed. He suddenly realized he felt part of a family.

He froze.

"Quinn, is something wrong?" Molly asked as she dumped the remains of the dessert into the trash bag.

His gaze flew to her face. "No! No, nothing at all. How long does the party last?" The sudden urge to escape had nothing to do with the party—and a lot to do with the panic filling him.

"If you need to leave, we can manage. You've been a big help. I appreciate it. Just tell Sara you have to go back to work."

Her easy acceptance of his need to escape surprised him. And calmed him. Molly wasn't trying to trap him into anything. In fact, she'd encouraged him not to come. And now that he was here, she wasn't demanding he stay.

"No, I just wondered. It's hard to believe they can keep this energy level going for so long."

"Now that they've had sugar, they can go for several more hours." The rueful smile on her beautiful lips made him want to kiss her. He took a step backward.

"Quinn? Just tell Sara—"

"I'm not going anywhere," he assured her, even

though he was shaking inside. He'd never been attracted to a mother before. But then, Molly was an exceptional mother.

He'd get over it. In fact, better that he stay. She'd get ornery when the children continued to be so demanding. He was sure she would. Better to see her feet of clay than to leave now, thinking her perfect.

WHEN SHE HAD THE CHILDREN seated in a circle on the rug, Molly handed the first present to Sara, hoping her daughter remembered the rules she'd drummed into her last night.

The first gift was a picture puzzle. "Oh, look, Mommy! A puzzle! I love puzzles. Thank you, Margaret."

Pride swelled in Molly's heart. She smiled at her daughter and nodded.

Sara began to get a little giddy as the presents piled up. She'd never received so much at one time. Molly carefully tried to keep her in check, reminding her of her manners when she forgot.

Finally all the presents had been opened, even one from Martha, except for the large box Quinn had carried in. Sara eyed it with awe. "It's so big!" she squealed.

"Maybe it's a train!" Jeremy suggested.

"I think it's a big dog!" another little boy exclaimed, standing to spread his arms as far as he could. All the children began to speculate and the noise level rose in the room.

Molly suggested Sara rip off the brightly colored paper and reveal the gift before the guessing got out of hand. In no time, Sara had done so. Suddenly the room got quiet.

"A dollhouse, Mommy!" Sara whispered, excitement in her voice. "It's a dollhouse!" Suddenly she looked up from the box, seeking the giver.

Molly watched, her heart in her throat when Sara found Quinn, watching the proceedings from the table. She flew across the room and threw herself at him, her little arms folding around his neck. "Thank you," she exclaimed, her lips placing several kisses on his cheek.

"I'm glad you like it, sweetheart," Quinn assured her, hugging her back.

QUINN WAS HAPPY his present had been a success, though Sara's enthusiasm had dimmed slightly when she realized she couldn't open the box and take it out. The dollhouse was in pieces, waiting for someone to put it together.

Which explained why he was standing in the kitchen waiting for everyone else to leave. Pam had offered to take Martha home, for which he was grateful.

"Thanks for all your help, Pam," Molly was saying. "And, Martha, we're so glad you came."

"I wouldn't have missed it," Martha said.

Molly escorted the two of them to Pam's van, along with five of the children.

Quinn was pretty sure Molly had forgotten he was still there when she came back into the house, a tired look on her face. After feeding the children, serving cake and ice cream, supervising the unwrapping of presents, she had led the children in games.

Sara stood beside Quinn. "Wasn't that the bestest party ever?"

"It certainly was. And you were a very good hostess, little Sara."

"Mommy 'splained about being a hostess." Sara leaned against his leg. The sugar appeared to be wearing off and Sara looked tired.

Molly came back in. "Oh! I hadn't realized— Sara, did you thank Mr. Spencer for coming to your party?"

"Yes, Mommy, and for my bestest present, too. When can you put it together?"

Quinn smiled wryly at Molly's effort to remain enthusiastic about his gift. He knew she had a busy schedule between now and Sunday.

"I'm not sure, sweetie, but I'll do it as soon as I can," she promised.

"I have a better idea," Quinn said, watching Molly.

"What?" Sara asked, lifting her face to him.

He bent over and scooped her up in his arms. "How about you go lie down and take a—" he remembered just in time to use the right word "—a rest, and I'll work on the dollhouse. Maybe when you get up, I'll have it all put together."

"Couldn't I help you?" Sara asked, her arms around his neck.

Quinn swallowed, realizing how hard it was to remain firm when those big blue eyes were pleading with him. "Uh, I think Mommy wants you to have a rest."

"Quinn—I mean, Mr. Spencer is right, Sara. You've had a big afternoon. You need some quiet time." Molly crossed the room and took Sara from him. "And I suspect Mr. Spencer would like some quiet time, too. We'll get your dollhouse put together another day. You have lots of toys to play with until I do.''

''But, Mommy—''

''Sara.''

That one quiet word had Sara capitulating. ''Okay,'' she whispered, and put her head on Molly's shoulder.

As she walked toward the kitchen door, Molly said, ''If you need to leave, feel free to go. I appreciate all the help you gave me.'' With a small smile, she disappeared from sight, along with Sara.

Quinn surveyed the kitchen. Molly had kept up with the cleaning as the party progressed. Everything was almost shipshape. In fact, it was hard to tell a party had taken place. He could leave, knowing Molly would be able to rest.

But he wasn't leaving.

He took out two more paper plates and cut two pieces of Sara's cake. Then he added a scoop of ice cream to each piece and set them on the table, with spoons.

As Molly came back through the kitchen door, he was taking his first bite of the cake she'd made.

''Oh! I'm sorry, I forgot you didn't get any cake.''

''I hope you don't mind me helping myself,'' he said, offering a smile to charm her.

''Of course not.''

''I fixed some for you, too. You didn't have a chance to eat any, either.''

''I warned you children's parties are rather hectic,'' she pointed out as she sat down.

''Great cake.''

''Thank you.''

He watched her as she took her first bite of cake

and ice cream. "How did you learn to decorate a cake like that?"

"There are kits. It's easy. I like doing that sort of thing. I talked to Jenna about fixing a sign for Sunday, offering my services for birthday cakes or special occasion desserts."

"Are you sure you'll have time?"

"Yes, of course."

"Martha said you need a husband." He hadn't intended to tell her about that remark, but it still bothered him.

Molly froze, a bite halfway to her mouth. She put the spoon back on her plate. "Martha's wrong." She shoved away the plate in front of her.

"Hey, I didn't mean to ruin your appetite."

She stood and carried her plate to the sink, scraping the remains of the cake and ice cream down the disposal and tossing the plate into the trash.

"You didn't. I want to thank you for coming today. It meant a lot to Sara to have you and Martha here. And the dollhouse is a wonderful gift. Too expensive, of course, but I can't make her return it. It would break her heart."

"Return it? Of course not!" he exclaimed, alarmed at the thought."

"Well, thank you." She stood, staring at him, and he realized she was waiting for him to leave.

"You're welcome. And I have a bargain to make with you." He wasn't sure she'd agree, but something insisted he try.

"A bargain?"

"Yeah. I'll stay and put the dollhouse together, if you'll feed me more chicken casserole when I'm finished."

"Oh, no, that's too big an imposition!" she exclaimed.

"Are you kidding? I'll enjoy myself, and I know you don't have time to put it together with everything you have to do for Sunday."

"Sara can wait for her dollhouse until next week," Molly protested, her jaw squaring. "It will teach her patience."

He cleared his throat. She wasn't going to make this easy. "Patience is important to learn, but I feel responsible since I got her the dollhouse. Consider it part of my gift."

"But I have things I need to do. I can't—"

"My point exactly. You do what you have to do, and I'll put the dollhouse together. You don't need to entertain me."

She stared at him, as if weighing his words, and he waited, wondering if he'd convinced her. Not that he intended to give up.

"Fine," she finally agreed with a sigh.

He was only being responsible, he assured himself. There was no reason to feel so relieved, as if he'd been given a reprieve.

He finished his cake and ice cream and carried the plate to the trash. "Great. I'll get started. May I use the table?"

"Of course. I'll wipe it off first."

In no time, he was seated at the table, the box open, trying to read the ridiculous instructions. He was convinced they'd been written by a sadist.

Molly worked at the sink, doing the last of the cleanup. She was close enough that he could ask her what she thought the words meant. When she came to look over his shoulder, he breathed in her scent, feeling warm and comfortable.

And excited.

THE AFTERNOON WAS a unique experience for Molly. She worked in the kitchen while Quinn put together the dollhouse, casual chitchat interspersed with comfortable silence.

She'd seldom shared anything other than sex with Christopher. He'd dropped any pretense of enjoying her company once he'd realized her father wasn't going to share his money with him. Not that her father had been wealthy. He'd been comfortable.

When he'd died the year before Christopher's accident, she'd realized her situation and had put her inheritance in a certificate of deposit that Christopher couldn't touch. But in the end, she'd had to use the money to pay off debts after Christopher's death. So he'd gotten the money he'd wanted anyway.

Spending the afternoon with Quinn, sharing insignificant observations or offering suggestions, was quite an experience.

"What are you making now?" he asked her as she filled various-sized cake pans.

"A Christmas tree cake. I'm going to stack it, each layer smaller than the one beneath. With green icing and decorations, it should resemble a tree."

"That's clever," he assured her with a grin. Then he held out the directions. "Look at this. Do you suppose this is slot M?" he asked, and she stepped over to the table again.

"I think so." She stepped back, hesitant to remain too close to him, and studied the dollhouse. "You're almost finished with it. Sara will be so excited."

"I enjoyed seeing her face when she unwrapped it," he said, a reminiscent smile on his lips. "What does she want for Christmas?"

"We haven't had a chance to discuss Christmas, there's been so much going on. But I imagine we'll visit the Santa at Gates Department Store soon. The other children will remind her."

She went back to work on her cake.

"Does it ever scare you?"

His question brought her around to face him again. "What are you talking about?"

"The responsibility of being a parent. Does it ever scare you?"

Molly drew a deep breath. "Yes. The other day, when she was running such high fever, I was afraid I wouldn't do the right thing. Fortunately, I had some help that day. And I do appreciate it."

"I'm glad I could help." He appeared to be concentrating on the dollhouse, so she turned back to the stove.

"You said her father ignored both of you. Why? If he didn't want to be married, why— Did you get pregnant before the wedding? Did you force him to marry you?"

## Chapter Nine

Molly spun around and glared at him. "No! I did not force Christopher into marriage. And this is none of your business."

"I know it's not, but I'm trying to understand. I mean, you heard me say I had no room for children. That's a decision I've made because— Well, for personal reasons. But he married you. Why?"

She shrugged her shoulders as she turned her back on him. "I'm not sure. He thought my father had a lot of money and he desperately wanted to live in the fast lane. I think, early on, he was attracted to me. Until I agreed to marry him. Then the challenge was gone." She paused, then said in a low voice, "And Sara…Sara was a mistake as far as Christopher was concerned. He'd had too much to drink and woke me up and…"

"He wasn't a nice man, was he?"

"No."

"So you regret your marriage?"

"Yes, but never Sara. I could never regret my little girl. She's my reason for living."

"My mother didn't feel that way."

Molly's gaze sharpened. Quinn seldom mentioned

his family, and he'd never said anything about his mother. "How do you know?"

"She left when I was a little boy. Ran away with her lover."

"You haven't tried to contact her?"

"Seth had a friend look into it. He just told us she died twenty-three years ago."

"I'm sorry."

Quinn shrugged his shoulders. "It doesn't matter."

The kitchen door swung open and Sara stood there, staring at the dollhouse. "Look! It really is a dollhouse. Thank you, Mr. Spencer!"

"Perfect timing, Sara, my girl," Quinn assured her. Sara ran to his side and he lifted her into his lap. He handed her the mother, father and two children that came along with the house. "Here's the perfect family to live in your dollhouse."

Sara held the woman doll, one finger stroking her hair. "Look, her hair is the same color as mine and Mommy's."

"You're right," he agreed. "And the daddy's is dark."

"Your hair isn't dark," Sara said, looking up at him.

"That's true, but then I'm not a daddy."

"Why not?"

"Sara," Molly said, a warning tone in her voice.

"But, Mommy—"

"Do you want your dollhouse upstairs or here?" Molly asked, hoping to distract Sara.

"Can I keep it on the table?"

"No, we have to eat at the table. You can put it on the floor over by the television so you can play with it while you're watching some of your shows, if you'd like.''

''Okay.''

''I'll carry it for you,'' Quinn said, standing.

The pair crossed the room. Molly was surprised when Quinn sat down on the floor with Sara. Much to her surprise, he played with Sara and the dollhouse for almost an hour.

''Are you two ready for dinner?'' she finally asked.

''I'm hungry,'' Sara agreed. ''Can I have some more birthday cake?''

''Only if you eat your dinner first. Come set the table.''

When Quinn began to help, Molly protested. ''Quinn, you're a guest. Sara will—''

''We're a team, aren't we, Sara?'' Quinn asked, grinning at Sara. ''So I'll help.''

It wasn't until they were almost through dinner that Sara asked the question that must have been on her mind. ''If the family in the dollhouse is perfect, what are we?''

QUINN FELT THE SIZE of one of the dolls. How could he have made such a thoughtless remark? It reminded him of his decision: He wasn't cut out to be a parent.

''I didn't mean—'' His gaze flew to Molly, hoping she'd bail him out.

''Mr. Spencer meant that two parents and two children are a normal family, sweetie. It doesn't mean other kinds of families aren't okay, too.''

''What other kinds?'' Sara asked, watching her mother.

''Well, like you and me. Or other families that

only have one parent and more than two kids. There are families where there are stepparents, or adopted children, or…or any combination.''

''Are they perfect families, too?''

''Yes, they are.'' After studying her daughter's expression, Molly added, ''You know the quilts the ladies made for our bedrooms?''

Sara nodded, but she looked confused. Quinn could understand that emotion, because he was feeling the same way. What did quilts have to do with families?

''They're beautiful, aren't they? But, really, quilts are made from leftover pieces of material. They're like families. They're called patchwork quilts because they take a new form, different from before, but they're beautiful and useful. Families start out one way, but they grow and change. It doesn't keep them from being perfect. Just different.''

Quinn stared at Molly, wondering how she'd gotten so smart about people.

''Do you have a perfect family?'' Sara asked, staring at him.

Surprised by her question, Quinn was even more surprised by the laughter that rumbled through him. ''No, angel, I don't. My mother went away when I was little. So it was me and my brothers and my dad.''

''You didn't have a mommy?'' Sara asked, horror in her voice.

Quinn seldom mentioned his mother's departure. Now, twice in one day, he'd found himself talking about it. Sara's concern for him felt good. He reached over and hugged her tightly against him. ''No, but I had a pretty good dad.''

Sara nodded, then pointed out, "I don't got a daddy."

"I know, but you have a great mommy."

The child beamed at him and then her mommy. "She's the best."

"Thank you, sweetie. Now, finish your casserole so you can have a piece of your birthday cake."

Quinn had intended to leave as soon as dinner was over. After all, he'd spent a lot of time with Molly and Sara. He figured by then he'd be tired of the domestic scene.

Maybe it was the uniqueness of the day.

Or the charm of his companions.

Or the warmth of the house on a cold day.

But he found himself reluctant to depart.

He could've gone to a concert in Chicago. He'd been invited to a party in Madison. There were several parties in Green Bay before the Packers game on Sunday.

Instead, he chose to remain in Molly's home. He and Sara helped Molly decorate the Christmas tree cake, experimenting with different edible decorations.

When it was finished, Sara clapped her hands. "When are we going to have a real tree, Mommy? Shouldn't we have one before Sunday?"

Molly laughed. Her calm amazed him. After his first several encounters with her, he would've thought she'd go to pieces at the slightest hint of difficulties. Instead, she'd been strong and reassuring.

"No, my darling child, we won't put up the Christmas tree before Sunday. We'll wait until almost Christmas. That way the tree won't dry out."

"Did we have a tree last year? I don't 'member,'' Sara said, a puzzled look on her face.

"No, we didn't, because we were getting ready to move. Everything was packed away," Molly reminded her. "We were still living in Chicago. Do you remember that?"

Sara shook her head. "But I like it here."

"Me, too."

Quinn found himself startled to realize how much he liked Molly and Sara being there, too. Two weeks ago, he'd scarcely been aware of Molly's existence, and then only because Jenna was doing work for her. He hadn't even known Sara existed.

Now they seemed an important part of his life. A widow and her daughter. It amazed him, because he'd always avoided Molly's type. A nester. And he'd definitely kept his distance from children.

What was happening to him?

Sara yawned and Molly looked at her watch. "Oh, my, we've been so busy decorating the cake, you've missed your bedtime, young lady. Time for you to go to sleep."

"I'm not tired," Sara said, but since she yawned in the middle of her protest, Quinn was pretty sure her mother wouldn't believe her.

With a grin, Molly ushered her daughter to the kitchen door, telling her she'd have to take a very fast bath tonight.

"Can Mr. Spencer read me one of my new storybooks tonight?"

Molly turned to stare at him as if she'd forgotten he was there. "Um, no, sweetie, he—"

"Of course I can. I was hoping you'd ask because I like that dinosaur one," he said.

"Me, too!" Sara said, beaming at him. "I'll be really fast." And she ran out of the kitchen without waiting for her mother.

"Quinn," Molly said, "You don't have to—"

"Yes, I do. I promised Sara. I'll go find the book and get ready to read while you bathe her."

MOLLY, AFTER TIDYING the bathroom from Sara's bath, slipped into her daughter's bedroom. She discovered Quinn sitting on the floor beside Sara's bed, his back propped against the mattress, with Sara cuddled in his lap, the two of them absorbed in the story about dinosaurs.

She fought the feeling of being excluded. Normally she didn't have to share Sara's attention. Was she holding her daughter too close? But the fear she felt at trusting her daughter to a man, a man who might lose interest in Sara and break her heart, couldn't be dismissed.

And she didn't trust Quinn Spencer, playboy extraordinaire, to hang around. Even though he'd shown no impatience with small-town life since she'd met him, she knew his reputation.

"The end," Quinn pronounced.

"Read it again!" Sara pleaded.

Molly stepped in before Quinn gave in to her daughter's request. "No, Sara. It's bedtime. Thank Mr. Spencer and hop into bed."

Instead of a simple thank-you, Sara threw her arms around Quinn's neck and hugged him tightly. "Thank you for reading my story to me. Miss Kaitlin is teaching me to read, but I like to listen most of all." Then she kissed him on the cheek and got into bed.

Molly stared at Quinn, wondering how he would react.

He stood and tucked the covers around her daughter and returned the kiss she'd given him. "Soon you can read to me and I can listen."

"Yeah," Sara agreed with a grin.

"Good night, Sara. Happy birthday," Quinn whispered.

"It's been the bestest birthday ever," Sara returned even as her eyes closed.

Molly stepped forward to give her daughter a good-night kiss as well, but she wasn't sure Sara was even aware of her touch.

After she followed Quinn from the room, he asked, "She's already learning to read? At four?"

"Not really read. Kaitlin is teaching them sounds of letters. They're learning a few words, like dog, cat. They only work on it for a few minutes each day."

"I'm impressed. I don't think I learned to read until second grade."

"The world is spinning faster and faster. Second grade is much too late."

"Are you sure that's not too much pressure?"

Molly led the way down the stairs. "I thought you didn't know anything about kids?"

"I don't, but I don't want Sara to— I mean, she should enjoy being a kid."

Molly groaned. "After today, you're worried about Sara enjoying herself? Come on, Quinn."

"True," he said with a grin.

"I want to thank you," Molly said as they reached the entry hall. "You helped make it a special day for Sara. I appreciate it."

"Does that mean it's time for me to leave?"

She stared at him, surprised. "I—I assumed...did you want a cup of coffee?"

"I'd love one before I go out in the cold."

He assumed the pitiful look Sara had perfected when she wanted something.

"Have you been taking lessons from Sara?"

He grinned. "I need to. That kid could talk me into almost anything with those big blue eyes of hers."

"I suspect she could take lessons from you. Rumor has it you get your way most of the time." She reached the kitchen and began preparing the coffeemaker. She was regretting her offer to make coffee.

Coffee wasn't the problem.

But spending more time with Quinn Spencer, without Sara's chaperonage, was a dangerous thing. She couldn't let herself come to depend on his support, his companionship.

"Don't believe everything you hear," he muttered.

His words reminded her of a comic strip she'd read that morning. "Do you ever read the comics?"

He frowned. "Yeah."

"There was one this morning that dealt with gossip. The two women—"

He nodded. "I saw it. That's K.J.'s."

Molly looked puzzled. "K.J?"

"Local boy made good. He's living in Chicago now, but K.J., aka Kurt Eber, grew up here in Tyler. He's good, isn't he?"

"Yes."

She turned to take down two mugs. "Do you need cream or sugar?"

"No, I take it black."

She found small chores to do while she waited for the coffee to perk. She didn't want to join Quinn at the table. Better for her to keep her distance.

But when she'd poured the coffee, she had no choice. She sat down across from him, searching for an impersonal topic of conversation. "The wind is certainly blowing tonight."

He eyed her over the rim of his mug. "When all else fails, discuss the weather?"

Her cheeks turned a bright red. "I heard it whistling. I thought maybe a storm was coming."

"Maybe. We haven't had a snowstorm yet. We frequently have a white Christmas." The smile that accompanied his words sent shivers down her back.

"I'm sorry you missed work today," she said, changing the subject. "I hope it won't make more work for you."

"I've put in a lot of time lately. I needed a break."

"I'm sure this isn't your normal break."

He leaned forward, his smile still in place. "Variety is the spice of life."

"Some people's lives are spicier than others," she muttered.

"There you go again, listening to the gossips."

"Are you telling me you didn't go to Paris for a week in September?"

"An old friend was having a birthday party," he explained.

"And New York several times?"

"Friends," he said. "I used to work there."

"Miami?"

"A friend asked me to help man his sailboat for a race."

"London?"

"What are you, a travel agent? Or maybe you've had a crush on me for a long time and I just didn't know." His grin was at its broadest. "If so, you only had to let me know, Molly. I find you charming."

He couldn't have said anything that angered her more. He found her charming. A momentary charm that would pass when more exciting venues invited. Just like Christopher.

"No," she said crisply. "I don't have a crush on you. The point I'm trying to make is that you lead a busy life."

"And you don't? You had Sara's birthday today and you're hosting an open house on Sunday. You've moved nonstop all day."

"That's different."

"I don't see how. I work as a lawyer. You work as a businesswoman and a mom. You're probably the busier."

"I don't travel the world. My friends are limited to those I've met here."

He took a sip of coffee and set the mug on the table. "Why are we arguing this? What difference does it make?"

"I'm trying to say I know you won't have time to visit much in the future. I'll explain to Sara." She stood and took her mug to the sink, pouring out the half cup of coffee that remained. She wanted this discussion to end.

Apparently Quinn was in agreement, because he followed her example. But instead of turning toward the door, as she hoped he would, he took her shoulders in his hands. "I imagine I'll see Sara Sunday. Won't she be here?"

"Yes, she'll be here."

"Then there's no need to explain anything to her." Then he shocked her by leaning closer and brushing his lips against hers. In spite of herself, her eyes closed.

But Quinn didn't leave after their brief kiss. Just as he had when he'd tasted her muffins, he took a second taste, his lips settling more firmly into place, his body pressing closer.

Molly almost cried at the sweetness of his touch. He kissed her as if she meant something to him. She knew better, she really did. But she hadn't been kissed like that in so long, she couldn't push him away. She wanted—but she couldn't have what she wanted. So she should push him away. And she would. In a minute.

Then, before she could do so, he ended the kiss without a word, took his overcoat and slipped out the back door, a goodbye thrown over his shoulder.

Molly stood like a statue, trying to recover her calm. How could one brief kiss have such an effect on her? Her knees were shaking and she hugged her middle, hoping to restore her equilibrium.

"It's just the shock of it," she told herself. After all, she hadn't kissed anyone other than Sara since long before Christopher died. And Christopher's kisses had never made her feel...treasured.

She dismissed that ridiculous thought. Quinn Spencer was an expert kisser, that was all. He probably made every woman feel that way. And then forgot them.

But that kiss clarified what she'd been doing during her conversation with Quinn over coffee. She'd known she needed distance from the man. Protection

for her emotions. By reminding him of his jet-set
world, she'd hoped to force him to go away.

Because she couldn't afford to risk her heart again.

THE COLD WINTER WIND WAS a stark contrast to the
warmth of Molly's kitchen. Quinn tried to blame the
shivers that he felt on the change of temperature. But
even before he'd gotten in his car and started the
motor, he felt the change in his breathing.

It had to be the kiss.

He'd intended a friendly kiss. A reaching out to
say thank you for the day. But once he'd tasted her,
he couldn't back away.

He'd only been thanking her for the dinner, the
invitation to the birthday party. Or congratulating her
on having raised such a perfect child. That was it.
Sara was a remarkable little girl. He wanted Molly
to know he liked spending time with Sara.

As he began backing out of the driveway, ruthless
honesty had him shaking his head. Okay, he was attracted to Molly. Too much attracted. After all, there
was no future in a relationship with someone like
Molly. He wasn't going to be tied down to a home
life, raising a child, running errands.

He had places to go, people to see. Important people.

So why was he staying in Tyler for the weekend?

Because Molly was his client, and he felt responsible for the success of the open house, since it had
been his idea.

That excuse worked. Excuse? Why did he need an
excuse? He'd stayed in Tyler more times than not
since he'd moved back. There had been a few trips,
but—

He needed an excuse because of his family. Because of his friends. Because of his reputation. If he was going to continue to protect himself from matchmaking, husband-hunting women, he needed to be thought of as a jet-setter, a man with no ties, no interest in ties.

Panic began to build in him.

But he could fix it. He knew just what to do.

All it would take was a phone call.

# *Chapter Ten*

Molly spent Sunday morning doing last-minute preparations in her kitchen. Today she and Sara would
skip the church services they usually attended.

"Is Mr. Spencer coming today, Mommy?" Sara
asked from across the room. She was playing with
the dollhouse he'd given her for her birthday.

"He said he was. However, sometimes something
happens that makes it impossible for people to do
what they intend to do." It was a convoluted warning
that she hoped her daughter would understand.

"I hope he comes. I want to show him my family."

Distracted, Molly said, "But he's seen the family,
sweetie. Remember? He played with you Friday evening."

"But I fixed it, Mommy. Yesterday, while you
were busy, I fixed it."

Molly raised her head and stared at Sara. "What
do you mean, you fixed it?"

Sara came running across the room, two of the
small plastic dolls in her hands. When she got close,
Molly briefly closed her eyes. She didn't need the
explanation Sara gave her.

Holding up the father and boy, Sara said, "See? I used my paints to make them look like Mr. Spencer."

The dark hair of the man and boy had been painted, not too neatly, a yellowish brown.

Molly swallowed, trying to think what to say. "Um, I see. Well, I guess they match the mommy and daughter, don't they?"

"Yes, but they look like Mr. Spencer. That's the important thing. So he can be the daddy."

Molly laid down the crescent roll she'd been wrapping around a small sausage and knelt to be eye level with her daughter. "Sara, Mr. Spencer isn't a daddy."

"I know, but he can be one if he wants. Then we'd be a patchwork family, like you said." She beamed at her mother, as if she'd made a great discovery.

Molly wanted to cry, but she pasted a smile on her face. "No, sweetie, Mr. Spencer is a friend. He's not going to be part of a family. At least not our family. He's only a friend."

Sara's smile disappeared. "But I want him to be. Can't you ask him, Mommy? I think he'd like to be part of our family."

"No, Sara, I can't ask him. And neither can you," she hastily added as Sara stared at her. She knew how her daughter's mind operated. "We're going to be our own family. It may be a small one, but it's an extra good one. Okay?"

"Okay," Sara agreed, but her face looked glum.

"It's time for us to eat a quick lunch and then go get ready. And I have a surprise for you," she added, glad she had something to distract her daughter.

"What?"

"I bought us both new dresses to wear. Yours is very pretty."

"A new dress? Where is it?"

"In my bedroom. As soon as we eat, we'll go upstairs and look at it. Put your toys away."

Fortunately, Sara seemed to forget her plan to expand their family as she stored the dolls in the dollhouse and ran back to set the table.

"Darling, I hope you're going to take me to a late lunch after we do this reception thing. I haven't seen you in weeks!" the svelte blonde gushed as soon as she got off the plane. She clung to Quinn's arm and smiled adoringly up at him.

"Um, Clarisse, I'm sure you'll find a lot to eat at the reception. Molly is a great cook."

Clarisse snuggled even closer. "Molly...such an old-fashioned name. Is she one of those sweet, grandmotherly types?"

Quinn couldn't keep from thinking about the last time he saw Molly, when he'd kissed her. "Uh, no, she's more the happy homemaker type."

"Oh, poor Quinn. No wonder you wanted me to come. Is she making a play for you, looking for a man to take care of her?" Clarisse fluttered her lashes at him. "I know how you hate that type. Fortunately for me, I have Daddy's money. I don't need a man to support me."

By that time, they'd reached the car, and he held the door open for his guest. Yeah, Clarisse Donald was fortunate, because she was no more equipped to be independent than Molly was to let someone else control her life. If she had to do without everything but food and water, Molly would before she'd let some man support her.

"I don't have to be back until Tuesday," she said as Quinn slid behind the steering wheel.

Damn. He'd made her reservations and had her on a plane leaving at five that evening. She knew that. "Unfortunately, I've got a very busy week ahead of me. I'm even going to have to work after I put you back on the plane."

"But I've already changed my reservation," Clarisse told him, triumph in her gaze.

He pulled out his cell phone and dialed the reservations number for the airline she'd flown on. It was the one he usually used. Even as Clarisse protested, he changed her reservation back to that evening.

When he hung up, she lamented, "But, Quinn, we're not going to have any time *alone!*"

"Sorry, Clarisse, but this just isn't a good time."

In fact, he'd already realized he'd made a mistake, bringing Clarisse in from Chicago for the reception. What had he been thinking? Molly wasn't interested in him.

But he'd panicked when he thought about that kiss. As casual as it was, had been intended to be, it had shaken him.

So now he was stuck with Clarisse for the afternoon.

When they reached the Victorian home on Ivy Lane, Quinn discovered they weren't the first to arrive. Numerous cars lined the quiet avenue.

After parking, he hurried inside, with Clarisse glued to his side. The entryway was crowded with people he'd known all his life. In particular, his two brothers.

"Hey, Quinn, where's Dad?" Seth asked. Jenna, his wife, wasn't in sight.

Quinn shrugged his shoulders. "I had to pick up Clarisse at the airport, but Dad had already decided he wouldn't come with me. I thought maybe you or Brady were picking him up."

Brady shook his head. "I thought he was coming with you."

"You both remember Clarisse, don't you?" Quinn hurriedly said as the woman stroked his arm.

Both his brothers nodded and greeted her, but their gazes returned to him, questions in their eyes.

He quickly asked, "Where's Jenna?"

Seth grinned. "She's giving tours of the suites upstairs."

Quinn couldn't hold back the next question. "And Molly?"

"In the dining room," Seth said. "That's where most of the people are, trying to taste everything. Brady pointed out the muffins."

"Yeah, she made bite-sized ones, but they taste just as good. And did you see that Christmas tree cake?" Brady asked, enthusiasm in his voice.

"Well, really, I had no idea hors d'oeuvres were so important to men," Clarisse said with an arch laugh that set Quinn's teeth on edge.

"She's a good cook," he responded simply. Then he took Clarisse's arm to move her in the direction of the dining room. "Come on, I'll introduce you."

"I'm in no hurry to meet Muffin Molly," Clarisse protested. "I much prefer the company of three handsome men."

"Don't call her that!" Quinn snapped.

Clarisse opened her mouth—to protest, he presumed—but all three men were distracted by new arrivals. Their father entered, accompanied by Lydia Perry, one of the quilters.

"Hello, boys," Elias said in a booming voice. "You know Lydia, don't you?"

Lydia's cheeks were bright red. It could be the cold weather, but Quinn figured it might be nerves. He stepped forward and kissed her cheek. "Of course we do. How are you, Lydia?"

"Fine, Quinn. Your father was kind enough to give me a ride today."

"Good." Clarisse tugged on his arm, and he made the introduction to Lydia.

"We're on our way to meet Mrs. Molly Homemaker," Clarisse said, "if you'll excuse us."

"Where is Molly?" Lydia asked, frowning at Clarisse's snide tone.

"In the dining room," Quinn said, suddenly reluctant to present Clarisse to Molly.

"Does she have any of those muffins?" Elias asked eagerly.

Clarisse rolled her eyes. "I can't believe you men are fixated on muffins."

"They're damn good," Brady said, staring at Clarisse, "and yes, Dad, she does. But there are lots of other good things, too."

"We'll go with you," Elias said, catching Lydia's hand in his. "Oh, your coat, Lydia. We'll get too hot."

"Quinn forgot to take mine, too," Clarisse said as she slipped off the full-length mink. As Quinn took it, she struck an obvious pose, waiting for his response. She was dressed in a cocktail dress, cut startlingly low over her breasts.

It was Brady who commented. "That's quite a dress, Clarisse."

"Better than muffins?" she asked, but everyone realized it wasn't a question they needed to answer. Clarisse obviously thought she knew their reply.

"No," Elias said without any pretense as he handed his and Lydia's coats to one of the women acting as assistant hostesses.

Clarisse arched her brows, then patted Lydia on the arm. "You poor dear. He's obviously past the age to—"

"Clarisse!" Quinn snapped, warning her not to go too far. Then he drew a deep breath and headed for the dining room, a sinking feeling in his stomach that disaster was in the offing.

MOLLY HAD WORRIED that her new dress wouldn't be appropriate, once she'd noted how it clung to her body. She'd bought it in such a hurry that she hadn't realized how faithfully it followed her outline. She hadn't worn a sweaterdress in years, but it had felt so good, so comfortable, she'd thought it would give her confidence.

Its cowl neckline framed her face without the discomfort of a turtleneck, and its royal-blue color was a favorite. As she greeted her guests, they seemed to approve of her choice, so she'd relaxed.

Until she realized the newcomers included Quinn with a beautiful blonde in a stunning dress. Suddenly she felt dowdy. "Good afternoon," she greeted the group formally.

"The place looks terrific, Molly," Quinn said in

a low voice with a smile. Then he added, "Let me introduce Clarisse Donald, a friend. You already know Lydia, of course, and this is my father, Elias Spencer."

Molly nodded to the blonde, kissed Lydia's cheek and offered her hand to Mr. Spencer. "I'm so glad all of you could come."

Clarisse was the first to respond. "Oh, I never turn down an invitation from my lover. Every minute I can spend with Quinn, even attending a reception—" she made it sound like torture "—is worth whatever I have to endure."

She snuggled up to Quinn and kissed his cheek.

Her message was so clear it could've been in neon lights. *Hands off, he's mine.*

Molly tried to justify the nausea she was feeling. The woman was too obvious to be believed. And the warning wasn't necessary. Molly had known Quinn wasn't going to have a role in her life. Other than legal.

"How nice," she said, ignoring Quinn's embarrassment. "Maybe after you look around, Quinn will take you somewhere more enjoyable." And she turned her attention to Elias Spencer and her friend Lydia.

Elias was explaining to her about his enjoyment of the muffins when Clarisse touched her arm, interrupting.

"I've embarrassed Quinn, so I'd better apologize. I didn't mean coming here was torture. At least—" she paused to giggle "—no more than anywhere else with a crowd. You know how it is when all you want is to be alone."

"Of course, I understood what you meant," Molly

said with complete sincerity. "Please feel free to cut the tour short and find somewhere you can be alone. Quinn has done his duty."

Then she resumed her conversation with Elias and Lydia, escorting them personally to the buffet displayed on the different tables.

"Isn't she horrid?" Lydia asked in a whisper.

Molly smiled but shook her head.

"Yeah, she is," Elias agreed. "I never have liked her. I don't know what got into Quinn, bringing her all the way from Chicago."

Molly was pretty sure she knew, but she wasn't going to contribute to this conversation. "Jenna is upstairs give tours of the two bedrooms I've finished, with the quilts in place. I hope you like them, Lydia. After you've sampled some of the food, be sure you see them."

"Oh, yes, I can't wait. Elias, Molly has decorated the bedrooms around our quilts."

"Then I know they're terrific. We'll go up as soon as I taste those little sausage things, along with the muffins. You've got to taste these muffins, Lydia."

Molly left them to greet other newcomers, but she was intrigued with the comfort level between those two. She hadn't heard that Lydia was dating anyone, but she was certainly an attractive woman. And Elias Spencer seemed much more at ease with small-town life than his son.

She forgot those two when she turned to the next arrival. Ursula Wilson stood glaring at her.

"Good afternoon, Mrs. Wilson. I'm so glad you've joined us," she said, smiling.

"It would certainly be hard to ignore you with all

the traffic and noise clogging our little street. I knew it would be like this!"

"This is a special circumstance, Mrs. Wilson. The Breakfast Inn Bed only holds ten or twelve guests at a time, not the several hundred who are visiting today."

"So you say now, but I'm sure you'll be wanting to expand before we know it, with your toe already in the door. Then it'll be like this all the time!"

"I don't think I could handle that much business," Molly said mildly, keeping her temper under control.

"Good, refer them all to us," a man said, laughter in his voice.

Molly was delighted to welcome Joe Santori and his wife Susannah. They ran the other bed-and-breakfast in town. She'd talked with them about being competition for the business and had found them delightful.

"Joe, Susannah, thank you for coming."

Susannah stepped forward to kiss her cheek, surprising Molly. "We couldn't miss it. Gina's been raving about the place since she interviewed you. She came with us, but she stopped to visit with some friends."

Molly's eyes widened. "Good heavens, I never put it together. You're related. I should've—"

Ursula Wilson snorted in disbelief. "Everyone knows Gina is their— Well, Joe's daughter. You can quit playing the innocent."

Molly's cheeks heated up, and she struggled to remain calm. "I guess I should have made the connection, but I've been reading Gina's column ever since I moved here, and I thought of her as someone famous."

Joe chuckled. "I'll have to tell her that. Of course, now you've offended Susannah."

Molly felt she was going down the tubes quickly. "I did? I'm sorry," she began, a frown on her face.

"Just ignore my socially inept husband," Susannah said with a chuckle. "He's referring to some books I've done on life-styles, but I don't expect them to appeal to everyone."

Molly shook her head, ashamed of her gaffe. "I didn't know. I'm so—"

"And so you should be," Ursula agreed, venom in her voice. "It just goes to show that an outsider shouldn't come into a community and try to compete with *our* people."

Molly realized they'd drawn an audience and felt sure the reception idea had been a disaster. She wondered if her business would survive.

"Compete?" Joe boomed. "Molly isn't going to compete with us. We're going to work together, referring people to each other's place when we get full. And looking around, it's going to be a pleasure, Molly. You've done a fantastic job."

There was a kind light in his eyes, echoed in Susannah's smile, that boosted Molly's spirits.

"Hear, hear!" Elias Spencer called, and began clapping. Everyone who'd been listening joined in.

"Have you tasted her muffins?" Elias added.

QUINN LEFT THE AIRPORT with a sigh.

What a mistake in judgment he'd exhibited. Clarisse had made the day so much worse than he'd expected. She'd done her best to embarrass Molly several times, particularly when he hadn't taken the hint and moved her away. But he wouldn't give in to that kind of pressure.

Nor would he allow her to force him into marriage. She'd intimated to everyone they met that they were lovers and had permanent intentions.

Not likely.

Well, he had to admit he'd slept with her a couple of times. She was an attractive woman who didn't mind using her body to gain social prominence. He'd succumbed before he realized her personality canceled out the sexy body she showed off.

That dress she'd worn today had shown her for-sale sign to everyone who looked at her.

Molly, on the other hand, had exhibited class, never more evident than when Ursula Wilson had attacked her. Quinn had been so proud of Molly.

But with Clarisse in tow, he couldn't say anything. It would only have drawn more venom to Molly.

Which was why he was headed back to Molly's right now. He knew she'd be tired after her afternoon, but the reception was supposed to have ended at three. That was two hours ago. He and Clarisse had left a little before three, and he had to admit the crowd hadn't thinned out, but he felt sure they'd all be gone now.

He was going to offer an apology for Clarisse's behavior and praise Molly for her handling of Ursula Wilson. When he'd suggested the reception, he hadn't envisioned an all-out attack on Molly, but she'd handled it so well, he felt sure public opinion would be in her favor.

He hoped she was still wearing that blue dress.

With a frown, he warned himself to keep his mind off Molly's appearance. But she'd looked so sexy, so...touchable, that he hadn't been able to ignore her. And he'd tried to watch to make sure the other men there didn't get too enthusiastic about greeting her. She didn't seem to realize how attractive she was.

Of course, Clarisse had drawn attention with her crass appearance, too, but Quinn figured she'd asked for whatever she received.

Not that anyone was rude. Or even interested. Clarisse didn't fit in Tyler.

Molly, however, was perfect.

For Tyler! Perfect for Tyler. Not for him, of course. He wasn't interested in marriage.

Visions of Molly, as she was dressed today, of little Sara, cute as a button in her party dress and so proud of it, filled his head. They were both special ladies.

Remembering the admiring looks in some of the men's eyes, coupled with Martha's remark about finding a husband for Molly, had Quinn pressing hard on the gas pedal.

He needed to make sure Molly was okay.

Just because she was a client, of course.

Nothing more than that.

# Chapter Eleven

"I insist," Jenna said. I'm going to get a lot of business out of the work I did for you. And you shouldn't be cooking after all you've done today."

Jenna and Seth, her husband and Quinn's oldest brother, hadn't left yet. Jenna wanted Molly to go out to eat with them.

"I think Jenna's right," Elias Spencer agreed. He and Lydia were lingering also. "We can make a party of it."

"May I join you?" Eden Frazier, the florist who'd done the arrangements for the reception, asked.

Molly drew a deep breath. Her preference would be to withdraw to her bedroom and close her eyes, but it was clear that wasn't an option. "Of course you can," she said with a smile. "Your floral arrangements were perfect and added so much to the reception. I'd love for everyone to join us, as long as I pay for my and Sara's dinner. And as long as you realize a four-year-old will be there," she added, rolling her eyes.

"Good," Pam Kelsey said. "That way Patrick and I can bring Jeremy and join you, if you don't mind."

"You know I don't," Molly said. "In fact, maybe

I should buy your meals because it will make Sara so happy to have Jeremy with her.''

Patrick, his arm around his wife, objected. ''Don't even think of it. It will work for all of us.''

Brady, who had also been waiting, joined in, as well as Kaitlin.

''I hope we can find somewhere that can handle this big a crowd,'' Molly said, frowning.

''That's not a problem,'' Elias assured her. ''I'll call Marge and tell her we'll need her back room. She keeps it for meetings and such. We'll call ourselves the Welcoming Committee for Molly and Sara.''

''But I've been here for almost a year,'' Molly protested with a laugh.

''Better late than never,'' Elias said with a grin and asked to borrow her phone.

While he was calling, she thanked her friends again for their support. ''I'm so glad Sara and I came here. I've never felt so much at home in my life.''

Their laughing responses only reinforced those feelings. When a knock sounded on the door, everyone grew silent. With a frown, Molly hurried to the door. Who could it be? Her friends were all there.

Along with a puff of cold air, Quinn entered the house as soon as she opened the door.

''Quinn!'' she exclaimed. Then, before closing the door, she peeked out, wondering what had happened to Clarisse. ''Um, where's your— I mean, Clarisse?''

''She's on her flight back to Chicago. I thought the reception ended at three,'' he said, staring at the crowd of people.

They all stared back him, but they didn't respond.

''These are friends who— We've been visiting.''

"And we're all going over to Marge's for dinner," Brady added. "We didn't think Molly should be cooking after all the work she put into the reception."

Molly didn't think Quinn looked too pleased about Brady's explanation, but he immediately invited himself to join them. No one really waited for Molly's approval. It was assumed she would agree.

And they were right. She couldn't say no. But she stepped away from Quinn. Eden or Kaitlin or…someone could keep Quinn company.

"I'll go get the kids and our coats," she said, turning to the stairs, hoping to escape.

"I'll help you," Quinn said, reaching her side before she could protest.

"No, that's not necessary. I'll only be—"

"I didn't get to see much of Sara today," he said, taking her arm and pulling her along as he started up the stairs.

When they reached the staircase to the third floor and she knew no one could hear or see them, she jerked her arm from his hold. "What are you doing? Why did you come back?"

"I owe you an apology."

"No, you don't."

"Yes, I do. I shouldn't have brought Clarisse. She wasn't nice to you, and you had enough to deal with without her complicating things."

"There's no need to apologize. She clearly felt threatened, probably because your father was being nice to me. She didn't realize it was my muffins that he was interested in."

"I don't belong to Clarisse. She's a friend, nothing more."

"Just friends" was such a trite answer and it meant absolutely nothing. She couldn't resist challenging him. "Oh, so you and Clarisse have never been anything but friends?"

It amused, and saddened her, to see his cheeks turn red. She wasn't an idiot. She'd seen how her husband Christopher had operated.

"At one time we— She means nothing to me now."

"And yet you invited her today." She'd reached the third floor. "Sara? Jeremy?"

Before Quinn could say anything else, the two four-year-olds popped out of Sara's room.

"What is it, Mommy?"

"We're going out to eat, so you need to get your coat. Jeremy, is yours downstairs?"

"Is Jeremy going, too?" Sara asked, excitement on her face.

"Yes, he and his parents are joining us."

"Whoopee," Sara cheered.

"Hey, what about me?" Quinn asked, stepping out of the shadows. "Aren't you excited that I'm coming, too?"

"Mr. Spencer! I didn't know you were here!" Sara ran forward and wrapped her arms around his legs.

He swung her up into his arms and kissed her cheek. "Sure I'm here. I came back to see if you and your mom were exhausted, but you look in pretty good shape, little Sara."

"And Mommy, too," Sara prompted him. "We wore our new dresses," she reminded him, patting the skirt of her green dress.

"I know, and you both looked extra-special," Quinn assured her, but his gaze traveled to Molly.

It upset her that his words could mean anything. What was he going to say, that she looked frumpy next to Clarisse? "Let's hurry. I'm hungry. Sara, get your coat and I'll get mine."

She hurried into her room, across the hall from Sara's room, glad to escape Quinn's presence.

When she turned back to the door, coat in hand, she discovered she hadn't escaped at all. Quinn stood in the doorway, looking at her room.

"What are you doing?"

"I wanted to see what your room looked like," he said with a shrug, as if invading her space was perfectly acceptable.

Every protest she could think of would make her sound small-town, provincial. She swallowed her nerves and moved toward him, forcing him into the hallway. Then she pulled the door closed, hoping it would emphasize her privacy.

When they got downstairs, Elias had returned from the phone, announcing Marge was delighted to open her back room. Marge's Diner had long been a favorite in Tyler.

"Well, hello, Quinn," he said as Quinn followed Molly and the two children down the stairs. "I didn't know you were here."

"Yeah. I'm joining the crowd."

Pam and Patrick asked if Sara could ride with them and Jeremy. Molly didn't have a problem with the offer, except that it left her without Sara as a chaperon. While Quinn talked to his father, she stepped to Kaitlin's side. "May I ride with you?"

"Sure. Eden and I are going to ride together, but there's plenty of room. Quinn isn't—?"

"No. Ready to go?"

"Sure. But don't you have to lock up after everyone's out?"

Molly chewed her bottom lip. She'd been in such a hurry to escape Quinn, she'd forgotten about that. "Yes. Help me urge everyone out."

She tried to keep her distance from Quinn even as she nudged everyone to leave. But he stubbornly waited by the door. When she, Kaitlin and Eden went through the door and she waited for him to follow, he stepped through and immediately said, "I'll drive you to Marge's."

"No, thank you, I already have a ride," she told him without looking at him.

He didn't hesitate to show his displeasure. "With whom?" he demanded.

"Kaitlin and Eden. You're going to give me a bruise!" she protested as his grasp had tightened.

QUINN WAS STUNNED that he'd lost control so quickly. But the thought that another man might've cut him out chased his common sense away. He immediately released her.

Before he could gather himself, she'd locked the door and hurried down the steps after Kaitlin and Eden.

"Say, Kaitlin, mind if I catch a ride? There's no reason to take so many cars, if you don't mind."

"Of course not," Kaitlin agreed with a good-natured smile.

In spite of Molly's rush, Quinn caught up with her and maneuvered her into the back seat with him.

He'd realized he wouldn't be sitting next to Molly at dinner if he didn't arrive with her. It was clear she wasn't in a friendly mood. She must be more upset about Clarisse than she'd said.

Which could be a good thing.

If he were interested, of course. As it was, he was just interested in her reactions because she was a client.

Right.

When they reached Marge's, he discovered Brady had saved four seats at the end of the table and waved to them as they came in. "Here you go!"

The next hour wasn't what Quinn had had in mind when he'd returned to Molly's house. The conversation was general, discussing the reception, leaving no opportunity to really talk to Molly.

"What did you tell Clarisse she was doing?" Brady finally asked. "She looked like she was attending the Oscars, exposing as much skin as possible. Tyler will be gossiping about her for years."

All eyes turned on Quinn. "I told her we were going to a reception. I had no idea she'd think it was a cocktail party."

"She looked very sophisticated," Molly said calmly. "Chicago society is different from Tyler."

"And I know which I prefer," Elias said.

It struck Quinn that he did, too. If a stranger asked anyone in Tyler, they'd say Quinn liked a more exciting life than Tyler offered. He'd worked to build that reputation.

But he was finding it harder and harder to dig up enthusiasm for his travels.

Seth laughed. "We can't all be jet-setters like my

little brother, Dad. Especially not when babies enter the picture.''

Quinn exchanged a look with Brady. They'd discussed their brother's marriage. It wasn't that they didn't like Jenna. They did. But she was a city woman, like their mother had been. They weren't sure she would stay, and they didn't want their brother hurt, as they and their father had been.

As if to mock his thoughts, Jenna laid her head on Seth's shoulder and a dreamy smile played about her lips. Her husband leaned over and kissed her.

"Break it up, you two," Brady warned, "or we'll pelt you with the chocolate pie."

"I can't believe you ordered pie," Kaitlin exclaimed, changing the focus of the conversation. "Where does it all go? Every time I saw you at the reception, you were stuffing your face."

"Hey, I wanted Molly to think everyone appreciated her cooking," he said with a big grin. "Think how hurt she'd have been if no one ate anything."

Jenna laughed. "I don't think that was a problem. I couldn't believe how fast the food disappeared. And she'd cooked tons. Molly, did you get any nibbles for bakery products?"

"Yes, Jenna, quite a few. Your sign was terrific."

"I still think you're trying to do too much," Quinn muttered.

Molly lifted her chin. "And it would be your business because…?"

She smiled, but Quinn didn't think anyone was fooled. She wasn't happy with him.

"Whoa!" Elias exclaimed, a big grin on his face. "Son, I think you've met a lady who isn't impressed with your reputation. Good for you, Molly."

Several other people teased both Molly and Quinn. He pretended to be amused, but inside he was seething. What was the matter with her? He was only trying to be helpful. And he'd already apologized for Clarisse.

When Molly, a few minutes later, asked for the check so she could get Sara home and tucked in bed, Elias told everyone he'd made arrangements with Marge to pay for the celebration. "After all, I'm the patriarch here. And, Molly, don't you dare protest."

Quinn decided he needed to learn to control things like his father. And he also needed to do a little investigating about his father and Lydia Perry. He didn't have any objections. In fact, his father had suffered longer than he should have because of his wife's desertion.

But he had some other probing to do this evening.

MOLLY GATHERED A SLEEPY SARA close as she rode in the back seat of Kaitlin's car to her house. As she got out, she thanked Kaitlin for the ride, told Eden and Quinn good-night and hurried up the steps to her porch.

As she inserted the key in the lock, putting Sara down momentarily, Quinn swung the child into his arms. "I'll carry her up."

She hadn't even realized until that moment that Quinn hadn't accepted her dismissal. "No! No, that's not necessary. You're not that sleepy, are you, sweetie?"

She should've known better. That turncoat Sara smiled sleepily and said, "I like for Mr. Spencer to carry me."

Molly ducked her head and led the way into the house without protest. It wouldn't do any good.

After they'd reached Sara's bedroom, Molly asked Quinn to excuse them while Sara put on her nightgown. After tucking her daughter in, she emerged from Sara's room, her fingers crossed that Quinn had left.

Instead, he was leaning against the wall and asked if he could tell Sara good-night. When he came out, she led the way down the stairs in double time, trying to keep her distance.

As they reached the entryway, he said, "I don't suppose I could get you to offer coffee? It's cold out there."

Rigid, she kept her gaze on the floor. "I'm afraid I'm too tired tonight."

"I figured," he said softly.

Her head snapped up and she stared at him. "What do you mean?"

"It was a busy day," he said.

She relaxed. Of course, that was all he meant. She'd overreacted.

"And you're angry at me. But I don't know why. I already apologized for Clarisse. What else did I do?"

"Nothing, Mr. Spencer. Thank you for calling. I'll let you know if I need any more legal help."

His hands shot out and grabbed her shoulders and he gave her a small shake. "Don't give me that formal crap, Molly Blake. We're not strangers."

"You're wrong. That's all we are, and all we'll ever be. So, good night, Mr. Spencer."

She'd hoped her formality would have an effect on Quinn. And it did. Just not what she'd hoped for.

He pulled her against him and his mouth covered hers. But this kiss was no light touching of lips, no casual salute. Instead, his mouth urged her to open to him, to share an intimacy deeper than Molly had ever experienced.

She intended to resist. Of course she did. But the warmth, the wanting, the wonder of his kiss, ruled out common sense. It must've ruled out sanity, too, because her arms slid around his neck, and she pressed even closer than before.

When he finally lifted his mouth from hers, the only thing he said was her name before he reslanted his lips over hers and kissed her more deeply. Molly's overcoat had been shed in Sara's room when she was putting her daughter to bed, so his hands were free to roam her sweaterdress.

She felt his touch through the soft material and it stoked the fire that blazed in her, long hidden beneath the disgust she'd felt for her husband.

Her body clamoring for more, she didn't even protest when his hand covered one breast and then the other through her dress. Lightning seemed to strike her and she moaned.

"Molly, Molly," he whispered, before kissing her again. She couldn't get enough of him.

"Come on, sweetheart," he panted. But he didn't finish those words. He couldn't seem to stop kissing her for more than a word or two.

"Upstairs," he urged, moving her toward the stairs as his hands began tugging her skirt up. The words put out the fire that had been raging through Molly.

Upstairs, where Sara was.

"No!" Molly protested, ripping herself out of his embrace.

A strange silence fell. Strange because Molly's body was protesting the free fall from ecstasy, while her mind was protesting her loss of control.

"Sweetheart, what— We want each other. You can't deny that," he protested, his breathing shallow, his voice husky with desire.

"No, but the answer is still the same. Please leave."

"Molly—"

Much to her shame, her eyes filled with tears. "Please!" She hated to plead, but she couldn't take any more.

Her weakness, as she saw it, had more effect than anything else. He reached out and cupped her cheek, but she flinched. His hand fell to his side and he turned and walked out of her house, saying nothing else.

Molly stood with her head down for several minutes before she crossed to the front door and locked it. Then she sank down on the bottom stair and sobbed into her hands.

She'd almost forgotten the cruel lessons of the past. She'd almost risked her daughter's happiness for—for incredible sex. She knew, without ever experiencing it, that Quinn's lovemaking would be unbelievable. He'd already stirred her more than her husband ever had. And all they'd done was kiss with their clothes on.

Only because she'd stopped him.

If she hadn't come to her senses, in five minutes, she would've been lost. Then both she and Sara would suffer heartache and abandonment again. Only this time it would be worse because they'd want so much more.

How could she have forgotten so quickly?

And what was she going to do about it now? She was committed to Tyler, to her bed-and-breakfast, to building a safe, secure home for her little girl.

Could she hope Quinn would decide to return to his world-roaming days, his sophisticated women? Would he realize, as she did, that tonight had been a mistake?

She slowly rose and dragged herself up two flights of stairs to her solitary bedroom.

But her personal space didn't offer the comfort it usually did. She couldn't shut Quinn out. He'd already seen her room earlier in the evening. But now he was in her head, in her blood. She couldn't forget his touch.

She couldn't save herself from heartbreak.

But she could save Sara.

And that was what she had to do, no matter how much it hurt.

# Chapter Twelve

Quinn rubbed his eyes and tried again to concentrate on the legal language in the contract he was supposed to approve for one of his clients.

Before he knew it, however, he was picturing Molly in the royal-blue sweaterdress that faithfully outlined her body. The body he'd caressed the night before.

"Quinn?" Amanda Trask, his partner, called as she rapped on his door. Before he could answer, she opened it and stepped inside. "Do you have— What's the matter with you? Are you sick?"

"No! I'm fine." He drew a deep breath and straightened his shoulders. "What do you need?"

Instead of answering right away, Amanda stepped closer and stared at him. "Hmm, Clarisse must've been very demanding last night."

"Probably, but not with me. She returned to Chicago on the five-o'clock flight." Again he asked, "What do you need?"

Amanda sat on the corner of his desk. "Then who put those shadows under your eyes?"

"No one. I didn't sleep well last night. Probably had too much caffeine. I'll cut back this evening."

He hoped he'd satisfied his partner's curiosity. "The open house was a success, don't you think?"

"Very much so. I hadn't seen the inside of the house since before old Mrs. Blake died. Molly certainly gave it a face-lift. It didn't hurt, of course, that she was smiling and friendly. That's another change from Mrs. Blake. Molly is such a darling, isn't she?"

"Um, yeah...darling."

"Oh, that reminds me. I got a call from the County Clerk's office. They've set the hearing for the zoning this Thursday evening. Molly will need to be present. I've got to call her. Maybe I'll ask Mrs. Allen to make the call because I'm already running late. I needed to—"

"I'll call her." He couldn't believe he'd offered to have more contact with Molly. About midnight, after staring at the walls of his bedroom for several hours, he'd decided he'd avoid the woman at all costs.

Amanda smiled. "Oh, good, thanks. I'll make a presentation to the City Council, of course, but they'll probably have questions for Molly. Would you have time to prep her on any possible questions?"

"Sure."

"Great. I'm leaving on the five-o'clock flight today, but I'll be back Thursday about noon. In plenty of time."

"Right," he agreed, and said goodbye as his partner responded to their secretary's prompting.

Then he bowed his head, resting his forehead on his fists in the center of his desk. First a phone call, then a prepping for the hearing. Which meant he had to see Molly.

"But it's business," he reminded himself. "Just business."

He reached for the phone.

When she answered, he almost forgot to speak as emotions flooded him.

"Hello? Is anyone there?"

"Uh, Molly, it's me, Quinn."

After a pause, she said, "Yes?"

"Amanda asked me to call." He wanted it understood up front that this was not a personal call. He kept his voice stiff and formal. As she had tried to do last night.

"Is something wrong?"

"No. But the date for the hearing has been set. It's Thursday night. Amanda wanted to give you plenty of notice. But she was running late and had to go to Chicago this afternoon."

"But—"

"She'll be back in time for the hearing. But I'll need to go over possible questions with you so you'll be ready."

"No! That won't be necessary. I'll be prepared."

"It's my duty as your legal advisor to prep you. There might be things you haven't thought of, and you have to be prepared," he warned. Why was he pushing for what he didn't want? *Because I'm a professional. I always do a thorough job.* It had nothing to do with what had happened last night.

"Make a list of questions and leave it with your secretary. I'll pick it up tomorrow."

"No. This has to be done in person."

"My schedule is too packed today. I can't—"

"I'll take you to lunch at Marge's tomorrow while Sara's in school. We can talk there." Then he could see her without being tempted to lose control. Which wouldn't do at all.

Apparently Molly thought the same thing because, after a moment's silence, she agreed.

"Fine, I'll pick you up at eleven-thirty."

"I'll be ready."

Her brief response brought a picture of her standing by the door so he wouldn't have a chance to come in. She didn't wait for his response but hung up the phone.

"Damn, you'd think I was a threat to the woman. All I did was kiss her!" he muttered.

"Did you call, Mr. Spencer?" the secretary asked, poking her head past his office door. He hadn't realized Amanda hadn't completely closed it when she left.

"No. I was talking to myself."

She waggled a finger at him. "Better be careful. You know they say people who talk to themselves are crazy."

"Thank you, Mrs. Allen. I'll let you know if I need you." To keep him from going crazy.

He picked up the contract still on his desk, to be sure the woman realized she was dismissed. When she disappeared, pulling his door closed after her, he breathed a sigh of relief.

Until he remembered that he had an appointment for lunch with Molly tomorrow. Then he forgot all about the contract.

By four o'clock, he'd given up trying to read the contract. His famous concentration skills had disappeared.

"No wonder. I didn't sleep more than two hours last night."

Damn it, here he was talking to himself again. He shoved the contract back into its file and left it on his desk. He'd try again in the morning after a good night's sleep.

Some cynical, sadistic voice deep inside him asked, "You think you're going to sleep any better tonight?"

He leaped to his feet and grabbed his overcoat. But he didn't bother with his briefcase. Tonight he was going to relax, take his mind off work…and off Molly. He could handle what had happened last night. After all, he'd been with more beautiful women. Certainly more willing. More his type.

Before the walls could laugh at him, he raced out of the office.

SILENCE REIGNED over the dinner table that evening until Brady showed up. Elias and Quinn had been eating their salads without any conversation.

"Well, aren't you two a chatty group," Brady said, as the housekeeper brought another salad and a place setting to the table.

"You joining us?" Elias asked, a smile on his face. Quinn hadn't bothered to smile and couldn't figure out what his father found to please him.

"I thought I would. Your housekeeper cooks better than I do, and I finished up early tonight." Brady turned to smile at Quinn. "I think your Molly has spoiled me. I don't like my own cooking anymore."

"She's not *my* Molly!" Quinn snapped.

Elias jerked his head up to stare at his youngest son. Before he could ask any questions, however, Brady spoke.

"Well, if you're not interested, maybe I'll visit

sweet Molly. She's going to make some man an incredible wife. He'd never go hungry.''

''Don't you think about anything but your stomach?'' Quinn demanded, leaping to his feet. ''Molly has a lot more to offer than her cooking.''

''After seeing her in that dress yesterday, I'd guess all the men in town know that, don't you think?'' Brady responded, winking at Quinn.

''Sit down, son, and finish your salad, or we'll never get to the roast beef Eva prepared.'' Elias sent a look Brady's way that Quinn couldn't interpret, but he wasn't finished speaking. ''I've been meaning to talk to you about Christmas.''

''Christmas?'' Quinn asked, lost. What had they said that made his father think of Christmas.

''Yeah, Christmas. It's only a couple of weeks away. I thought we might, uh, expand our guest list a little. Lydia doesn't have any family here, and I thought it would be nice to ask her to join us. You don't have any objections, do you?''

Brady and Quinn exchanged a look, but they both shook their heads.

''Good. We don't want Jenna to feel like the Lone Ranger,'' Elias said with a grin. His sons both stared at him, a lack of comprehension on their faces. ''The only female. That's what I meant.''

''Oh,'' Quinn said, still frowning.

''Good thinking, Dad,'' Brady agreed.

''Course, if you two would each find a lady, she wouldn't be the only female in the family.''

Quinn began to see a pattern. ''Brady and I aren't the only single men around here.''

Brady looked even more bewildered.

Quinn nudged him and nodded toward Elias.

"True," Elias agreed, showing no concern.

"Dad!" Brady exclaimed, shock on his face.

"Well? I *am* single."

Glad to have something else to occupy his mind beside a certain blonde, Quinn agreed. "You are, for way too long. Lydia is a nice lady."

"Yeah," Elias agreed with a warm smile on his face.

Quinn realized his father had been smiling a lot more lately. Was it because of Lydia?

"Anyway," Elias continued, "I thought you should ask Molly and her sweet little girl. It will get us used to having children around at Christmas. I need to practice, you know, because next Christmas we'll have Seth and Jenna's child."

This time it was Brady who encouraged his father. "Good idea, Dad. I know Molly doesn't have any other family, so she and Sara would probably enjoy celebrating with us."

"I don't think she'll come," Quinn snapped.

Elias eyed him curiously. "You two have a fight? Is that why you look like you didn't get a wink of sleep last night?"

"I had something on my mind," Quinn replied, avoiding looking at his family members.

"Maybe he was regretting Clarisse's departure," Brady suggested, a teasing look on his face.

Quinn didn't bother to protest. Let his brother think what he wanted as long as he didn't realize it was Molly, not Clarisse, who caused his insomnia.

"Well, you can invite who you want, Quinn," Elias said slowly, "though I'll admit Clarisse isn't a favorite. But I want Molly and little Sara to come. Will you take care of it for me?"

Quinn wished he could say no. But he couldn't unless he wanted to make some explanations that he'd rather avoid. Besides, he figured his father would ask Molly if he didn't.

"I'll extend the invitation, but I don't know if she'll come."

"Good enough." Elias rang the small dinner bell beside his plate. When Eva opened the door, he said, "We're ready for the roast beef now."

TWO IN THE MORNING. Quinn stared at the alarm clock, its numbers the only light in his bedroom.

"This is ridiculous!" he protested to no one. He'd stayed up until midnight, watching late-night television, but he'd found little to catch his attention. Then he'd turned out the lights, sure he'd fall asleep at once.

But he hadn't.

Now he understood why people got hooked on sleeping pills. Nothing was scarier than staring at the walls, knowing he needed sleep but unable to get it. Why? What was the problem? He'd gone without sex before. In fact, he'd practiced abstinence a lot more than most people would believe. Mindless sex had lost its attraction when he'd left the teenage years.

So why was it different with Molly?

Why couldn't he shut her out of his mind, dismiss her influence on his body? Get some damn sleep!

It was his fault.

He'd known he'd need to avoid seeing or speaking to Molly. That had been his game plan. But when the opportunity to call her had arisen, he hadn't been able to resist.

If anyone had asked, he would've assured him his

self-discipline was one of his strong traits. He may have played the playboy role, but in actuality, he'd worked hard on his career. He'd done what had to be done to not just survive, but to grow and succeed.

Except avoid Molly Blake.

He understood about withdrawal. You suffered a couple of days, then you continued with your life. But he'd agreed to see Molly tomorrow.

Agreed? Hell, he'd pressed her to meet with him.

"I was only doing my job," he muttered, but he had to be honest with himself if no one else. He'd wanted to see her. To see those big blue eyes that twinkled when she smiled. To let his gaze trace her soft curves. To breathe in her warm, wholesome but sexy scent. He craved those things as an alcoholic craved a drink.

And because he'd given in to his needs, he was spending another sleepless night.

With a sigh, he gave in to his wants and envisioned a smiling Molly, her arms around Sara. Then he imagined her in the kitchen, filling the room with fragrant odors, her curves wrapped in a big white apron, or in that sweaterdress that he couldn't get out of his mind.

It was hours till he finally fell asleep.

MOLLY HAD ACCOMPLISHED NOTHING with her morning. Except dressing for her lunch with Quinn. At first, she'd considered dressing as she had when she'd first met him: in stained, old clothes, her hair a mess, no makeup on. A silent message to tell him she didn't care about his opinion. But that would be cutting off her nose to spite her face. And it would be dishonest.

Besides, as a business owner, she needed to appear professional. And if she wanted people to believe her only reason for meeting Quinn was a business one, she had to look like a businesswoman.

So she dressed in a suit, a rich plum. It wasn't new, but she loved it. It gave her some much needed confidence. Then, holding her overcoat over her arm, she went down the stairs to sit on the bottom step, close to the door.

When she heard steps on her porch, she drew a deep breath, leaped to her feet and stood still until the knocker sounded. Then she shrugged on her coat as she opened the door. "I'm ready," she announced, turning away after permitting herself one quick look at Quinn.

Even as she stepped past him, she noted the dark circles under his eyes. She, too, had circles, but she'd hidden them with makeup. Her problem was caused by lack of sleep, since every time she fell asleep she dreamed of Quinn, of being in his arms.

She couldn't believe Quinn had lost any sleep over what had happened between them. Perhaps he was coming down with a bad case of the flu.

"Do you want me to drive my own car so you don't have to bring me back? I don't want to take you out of your way."

He gave her a disgusted look. "We're only talking a few blocks, Molly, not a cross-country trek. I'll drive."

She didn't argue. It was a business meeting. He'd stick to business. She'd known that when he'd called. His formality told her he was having second thoughts about what had happened.

He might want to take her to bed, but he didn't

want the strings that were attached to her. She knew he wouldn't be handling this chore if Amanda hadn't had to go out of town.

Marge's Diner was only half a block off the town square and was frequented by all kinds of people. At any time of the day one could see men in business suits, construction workers, women in jeans or suits.

And it always smelled of fresh coffee and good food.

Molly took a deep breath when she entered. It was nice to eat someone else's cooking.

A sandy-haired waitress showed them to a booth at the back of the L-shaped diner.

After the waitress left them with menus, Molly tried to cover the awkward silence. "I don't come in here often, but I don't remember seeing her before," she said of the waitress. "She's very pretty."

"She's been here a few months. I think her name is Caroline. She and Jenna both stayed at the Kelseys' boardinghouse together."

"Together? You mean they knew each other?"

"No. But they stayed there at the same time before Seth and Jenna got married." He folded his menu. "Want to know what's best?"

"Yes, please."

"The hamburger. It's big and tastes like a million dollars."

He actually smiled, a first for the day in Molly's presence.

"Okay, I'll have a hamburger," she said, hoping agreeableness would make the meeting easy.

"Then you have to have a piece of Marge's apple pie. They've even heard of it in Chicago."

Another smile. Whatever had been bothering

Quinn, it wasn't her. Since they'd arrived at the diner, he seemed quite at ease.

Caroline returned to their table. "Have you decided?"

"Yes, I have," Molly said. "Mr. Spencer has convinced me to have a hamburger."

"Good choice. And you, Mr. Spencer?"

"You know I told you to call me Quinn, Caroline. I'll have the same. How are things going? You decided to stay in Tyler yet?"

The woman's cheeks heated up. "I'm still deciding, but I do like it here."

"Smart woman. I'll take a cup of coffee right away, too. How about you, Molly? Want to warm up?"

"I'd love some," she agreed with a smile.

Watching Caroline walk away, Molly muttered, "Her hair is almost the same color as yours." It reminded her of the male dolls whose hair Sara had painted.

"A lot of people have sandy hair. I think it comes from our Scandinavian forefathers mixing with the heathens."

Molly wished he'd stop being charming. Since they'd come in and sat down, he'd been relaxed, entertaining. It was a wonder Caroline hadn't melted at his feet when he offered her that incredible smile.

It made Molly want him even more.

Stop it! she warned herself. Time to talk business.

"So what questions do you think I need to be prepared to answer?"

"Don't you want to wait until we've at least gotten coffee before we talk business?" His question was accompanied by another of those killer smiles.

She looked away. "Um, no, I think we should go ahead."

"First I'd like to know how Sara's doing."

"She's fine." She hadn't meant to sound so curt, but she didn't want this man to break her little girl's heart.

"Are you going to get all the quilts in time? You've only gotten two, haven't you?"

Why was he stalling? She would've thought he'd be anxious to get rid of her. "I talked to Martha yesterday afternoon. She thinks they will be. I hope the ladies aren't overdoing it, trying to have them ready by Valentine's."

"You're set on that as your grand opening?"

"Yes."

She looked up to see Caroline coming with two mugs and a carafe of coffee, steam rising from it.

When Quinn realized the waitress had arrived, he said, "Say, Caroline, you and Molly have something in common."

"We do?" she asked in surprise, pausing before pouring the coffee. "What?"

"You both like quilts. Jenna told me you have a terrific one."

Molly was looking at Caroline and saw the shock on her face. Then she was distracted when the carafe of hot coffee hit the floor and shattered, splashing the liquid everywhere.

# Chapter Thirteen

Caroline and Molly both screamed and Quinn gasped.

Marge came hurrying from the kitchen. "What happened?"

"I—I don't know. It just slipped out of my hands. I'm so sorry. Are you both okay?" Caroline asked, tears in her eyes.

Molly was dabbing at the brown stains on her suit but she stopped to assure Caroline she was fine. "It was an accident," she hurriedly assured Marge. "It's our fault, actually. We were talking to her, distracting her from her job."

Quinn nodded slightly at Molly's pleading look. "Sorry, Marge. We didn't mean to cause a problem."

"These things happen. Send me the cleaning bill for your clothes and lunch is on me," Marge said. "Caroline, go sit down for a few minutes and send Jimmy out with a broom and mop."

"Oh, no, I don't need to rest, Marge. It was my fault."

Marge ignored her protest as Caroline knelt to pick up pieces of glass. She motioned to the man peeking out of the kitchen, then turned back to Quinn and Molly. "Your lunch will be right here, and Alice will put you in a new booth and get you some coffee." Then she took Caroline by the arm and walked her back to the kitchen.

After they were reseated, Molly asked anxiously, "She won't fire her, will she?"

"Marge? Nope, she's a big softy. Besides, she knows it was an accident. Did it ruin your suit?"

Molly shrugged. "It doesn't matter. I've had it a long time."

Quinn gave her a crooked smile as he thought about how Clarisse would have reacted.

"Sorry about that, folks," Alice, an older waitress, said as she set down two mugs of coffee. "Didn't bring the pot with me. Thought it might make you nervous. But you need any refills, you just let me know. Marge said you get whatever you want."

"Thanks, Alice," Quinn said. "How's Caroline?"

"She'll be okay. Marge is making her eat some lunch and take a rest."

Quinn shot Molly a look that said "I told you so."

The cook called to Alice.

"I bet that's your order. I'll be right back."

Quinn grinned at Molly. "You're a cheap date, Molly Blake. I haven't bought you a meal yet, but you've fed me several times. Sunday night my dad paid, and today it's on the house."

The relaxed air, brought on by her concern for Caroline, disappeared and she turned rigid. "It isn't a date."

Quinn pressed his lips tightly together. Whatever charm had ever been attributed to him before, it had deserted him today.

Before he could find another way to put his foot in his mouth, Alice returned with their hamburgers. "Eat up, folks. You've got hot apple pie à la mode waiting for you."

"Thanks, Alice," Quinn replied. Molly never looked up.

As soon as Alice left the table, Molly, without touching her hamburger, said, "What do we need to cover for the hearing?"

"I'll start listing some things you need to think about if you'll start eating."

She shot him a stubborn look, but he continued to hold her gaze, not backing down. Slowly she picked up the hamburger and took a bite.

"Parking is sure to be a question that will come up. How many guests, on average, and where they'll park." He stopped and stared at her because she'd only taken the one bite.

With a huff of resentment, she took another bite.

"They'll probably ask about noise level, late-night revelry, music." He paused again.

Shooting daggers at him with her eyes, she picked up the hamburger.

"Since you added that card about baked goods, I'm sure there'll be questions about how much traffic that will incur, and whether or not you're licensed to sell baked goods."

"I assumed I'd be covered since I'm serving food to my guests."

"I would assume so, too, but I'll double-check that."

She frowned down at the table, not moving.

"How's the hamburger?"

She glared at him. "I'm eating! Is there anything

else?'' she asked as she lifted the hamburger to her mouth.

"There might be questions about advertising. And someone might be concerned about any competition you'll give the Santoris. They're very popular around Tyler.''

"Anything else?''

"Nothing that I can think of. You have any questions?''

"When are you going to eat *your* hamburger?''

He leaned forward, smiling, eager to smell her scent. "You concerned about my health?''

If he'd ever imagined any softness in her gaze, it definitely disappeared. "No, but I can't go back home until you finish eating.''

"You're a cruel woman, Molly.''

She never smiled, only nodded.

With a shrug, he took a bite of his hamburger. After chewing, he said, "I have something to ask you.''

He didn't know what she expected, but her eyes rounded in surprise.

"It's really my dad. He—he was very taken with you and Sara. He's inviting Lydia to Christmas dinner this year and he wondered if you and Sara would come, too.''

He saw a flash of pleasure in her face, but it quickly disappeared.

"Thank your father for the invitation, but I don't think we can make it.''

"Having hordes of family in for the holidays?'' he taunted, knowing she had no family. Damn it, he should just accept her answer, but he'd seen that look in her eyes. He knew how much she wanted family for her little girl. He wasn't going to allow her to deny Sara this treat.

She calmly took a sip of coffee. After setting down her mug, she said, "Is there anything else?"

"Yes. Dad wants Sara to come, and you know she would enjoy it." He almost pounded a fist on the table for emphasis, but they'd had too much excitement already with the exploding coffeepot.

"No."

"He wants to get used to having kids around because of Seth and Jenna's baby. He says he needs to practice. And it would be a lot of fun for Sara."

"I don't think it's a good idea. We're not part of your family."

"I know that. But we're having other people who aren't members of our family. Lydia certainly isn't. If we don't invite some other people, Jenna will be the only woman. Dad thinks that would make it difficult for her."

"Jenna isn't exactly a shy person, Quinn. I'm sure she'll be fine, and Lydia will be there." She paused, then asked, "Are you ready to go?"

"Not without my pie and ice cream. You can't go without tasting Marge's apple pie. She'll think you're a snob about baked goods, that no one can bake as well as you." Okay, so he was exaggerating, but as soon as they left the café, his connection to Molly would be ended. He could see it in her body language.

Alarm leaped into Molly's gaze, and he felt like a rat for making her worry about Marge. But it worked. "I'll have a small piece."

He waved his hand toward Alice and she hurried over.

"Ready for that dessert?"

"Just a small piece, please," Molly hurriedly said. "The hamburger was so large, I don't have much room for pie," she said with a smile.

Quinn grinned at Alice. "I'll have a piece, too. Marge's pie is too good to pass up."

Alice gave an enthusiastic nod and hurried to the kitchen.

Quinn was ready to start again on the invitation, determined to wear Molly down, when a big hand landed on his shoulder.

Elias Spencer said, "Didn't know you were eating at Marge's today, son. Hello, Molly. Good to see you again."

Lydia, standing beside him, greeted both Molly and Quinn with a smile.

Quinn slid out of the booth and stood. "Molly and I had some business to discuss, so we're combining work with lunch."

"Mind if we join you?" Elias asked. "We're just stopping by for a piece of pie."

Pleased at the opportunity to get closer to Molly, Quinn agreed immediately, sliding over to Molly's side of the booth. "No, we don't mind. Do we, Molly?"

"No, of course not," Molly agreed, as he'd known she would, but she pressed herself against the wall, getting as far from him as she could. It occurred to him that she'd be less likely to turn down his father's invitation for Christmas dinner, too.

Alice hurried back to greet the newcomers and take their order. When she disappeared again, Quinn took his chance. "I was just trying to convince Molly to accept your invitation for Christmas dinner, Dad."

"Oh, good," Elias boomed with a smile. "I'm looking forward to having friends join us this year. You and Sara will certainly brighten up the day. Does Sara still believe in Santa Claus? I was thinking of having one of the boys dress up in a Santa suit. Couldn't you do that, Quinn?"

Quinn blinked several times, surprised by his father's question. Even more surprising, Molly came to his rescue.

"I don't think that's necessary just for Sara. Besides, Santa will have already come to see her, and I certainly don't want an early start on next year."

Since she added a grin, Elias didn't seem upset. And Quinn wouldn't have to wear a Santa suit.

"Ah, you're right. That's why I need you to come, so I'll know what I need to do next year when we have a child in the family."

"Elias, the baby won't even be a year old," Lydia pointed out.

"Well, it'll be fun to have Sara there, anyway," Elias said. "What does she want Santa to bring her?"

"A doll and some storybooks. But Mr. Spencer, I—"

"Make it Elias, Molly. There's no need to be formal."

"Okay, Elias, I don't think Sara and I should intrude on your family Christmas."

"Bah! What intrusion? You'll be charming company. Lydia, especially, was excited when I told her you were coming. Weren't you, honey?"

Elias smiled at Lydia, so Quinn hoped he'd hidden his surprise at his father's pet name for Lydia by the time Elias looked at Molly again.

"That's very kind of you," Molly began.

Quinn could hear a "but" coming, but apparently his father couldn't.

"Good. But I'll tell you something. If it will make you feel better, we'd love to have you supply some dessert. Lydia is going to help Jenna prepare the meal, but I suspect Jenna won't be that much help. She's not domesticated like most women. They might not have time for dessert, too."

"We'd manage," Lydia protested, but then she smiled at Molly. "But it probably wouldn't taste as good as whatever you fixed."

"Of course I'd be glad—"

"Good. It's all settled then. Come around noon. We'll start with some appetizers and eat around one or so." He winked. "It depends on the football schedule," he joked with a grin.

"Elias Spencer," Lydia scolded, lightly slapping his arm. "Shame on you. Talking football on Christmas."

Quinn didn't care what they talked about on Christmas. But he was pleased that his father and Lydia had railroaded Molly into accepting the invitation.

THURSDAY EVENING, Molly had a few butterflies in her stomach at the prospect of attending the hearing. She'd been sleeping a little better, at least, because she'd been working herself to death, painting the other three suites until midnight the past few nights.

She wanted to have the rooms completely ready when the quilting ladies finished the quilts. With her intention of opening February 14 to emphasize the romantic nature of her Breakfast Inn Bed, it was important that she have everything done in time.

How ironic that she was making her living by promoting romance.

She immediately slammed shut that thought. Quinn must not be allowed to intrude into her thoughts tonight. She had to be on her toes.

"Mommy, Miss Kaitlin's here," Sara called up the stairs, excitement in her voice.

Kaitlin had volunteered to stay with Sara while Molly attended the hearing. To thank her, Molly had prepared dinner for the three of them. She hurried down the stairs.

She'd left Sara watching out the front window with instructions to call her when she saw her teacher arrive. "Thank you, sweetie. You did a good job."

Sara beamed at her. "I like Miss Kaitlin."

"I know you do. Did you finish setting the table?"

"Yes, Mommy."

She opened the door to Kaitlin. The air was cold, as usual, but the wind seemed to be blowing harder. She was glad she wore her wool slacks and heavy sweater.

"Ooh! I think it's getting a lot colder," Kaitlin said as she dashed inside. "I guess it's the snow."

Molly looked outside. "What snow? I don't see any snow."

"Didn't you listen to the weather report?" Kaitlin asked. "Oh, I guess you'd already picked up Sara, but Pam, when she came for Jeremy, said they'd warned them at school that there's a big storm coming tonight."

"What time tonight? Will we be able to hold the meeting?" She didn't want to have the meeting postponed. She'd been dreading it ever since Quinn had called.

"I think so. Attendance might be down a little, but they really don't think it will hit until late."

"Oh, good. Let's go to the kitchen. Dinner should be ready."

She'd prepared a savory stew, with hot rolls and salad. It didn't take long to put everything on the table.

"Mmm," Kaitlin said, sniffing the air as she sat down to dinner. "They should bottle that smell and sell it. It would attract a lot more men than perfume does."

Molly raised her brows. "Are you wanting to attract anyone in particular?"

Kaitlin grinned. "Who, me? They do make life a little more interesting, don't you think?"

"I think I'd rather have boring. Sara and I have already had our share of interesting because of a man."

"I'd like a daddy," Sara announced, proving she'd been listening to their conversation.

Kaitlin stared at Molly, leaving it to her to answer her daughter.

"Sweetie, we've talked about this. We're a team, you and me. We're not looking for a daddy." She added a bright smile and turned to pour a glass of milk for her daughter.

"But, Mommy—" Sara protested.

"Sara, we're not going to discuss this anymore right now."

Sara fell silent, but she had a stubborn look on her face that Molly recognized with dread.

"Sorry," Kaitlin said quietly.

"Don't worry about it. How was school today? Sara loved making her ornament, didn't you, sweetie?" Molly asked, trying to distract her daughter.

"But we don't have a tree yet," Sara reminded her.

"I know, but if the weather's not too bad, we'll get one Saturday, okay? Then you'll be able to put your ornament on it."

"But one won't be enough," Sara said, frowning, clearly worrying about their tree, which was a lot better than worrying about a daddy.

"We have some ornaments from other years, and I thought we'd go shopping for a special ornament for this year, too. Every year we'll each choose an ornament to hang on the tree."

"Can I get a Santa Claus one?" Sara asked eagerly.

"Whatever kind you want," Molly assured her. "Now, eat your dinner, because I made some cupcakes for dessert, but you can't have them until you've finished your stew."

"Bribery," Kaitlin muttered under her breath.

"You betcha," Molly agreed, "and I made enough cupcakes for your classes tomorrow as a treat. Is the bribe working?"

"You betcha," Kaitlin agreed with a grin, then joined Molly in laughter.

They were enjoying their meal a few minutes later when the doorbell rang. Sara had just spilled some of her milk and Molly was cleaning it up, so Kaitlin jumped to her feet.

"I'll see who it is."

Molly was grateful for the help, but she frowned

as Kaitlin left the kitchen. Who could it be? Everyone knew the hearing was this evening.

She finished wiping up the milk and turned to the sink to rinse out the cloth when she heard the kitchen door opening behind her.

"Who was—?" she began as she turned around. Then she stopped her question because Quinn Spencer was standing in the doorway behind Kaitlin.

"Mr. Spencer!" Sara shrieked, and dashed off her chair to hug his legs.

"Hi, sweetheart," Quinn responded, swinging her up into his arms so she could hug his neck. "How are you?"

"I'm staying with Miss Kaitlin while Mommy goes to a meeting. Can you stay with me, too?"

"No, I can't, baby. I have to go with your mommy to help her."

Molly stared at him. "I believe I can find my own way to the meeting."

Her inhospitable tone made Kaitlin stare at her as if she were a stranger. But what was Quinn Spencer doing here?

"I'm sure you could," he replied, "but I was worried about the storm that's supposed to come in tonight. Driving home might be rough, so I thought I'd do the driving for you." He gave her that easy, charming smile that always served him well.

She managed to produce a tight smile. "There's no need. I grew up in Chicago. I'm used to driving in the snow."

"Maybe so, but you shouldn't be out alone in a storm."

Kaitlin stepped forward. "You really should go with Quinn, Molly. Since he's already here."

Molly was boxed in, and she knew it. If she didn't make nice, Kaitlin was going to think she was horrible. "We'll see. Would you like a cup of coffee to warm you up?"

Quinn drew a deep breath. "I'd love one. And if you have any of that stew left over, I wouldn't mind it, either. I had an emergency at the office and missed dinner."

"Oh, you poor dear," Kaitlin said, taking his arm to urge him to the table. "You must be starved."

Molly would've held up a white flag if she'd had one. The man had done it again.

"There's plenty," she muttered. She always made a big pot of stew and then reheated it for lunches later. Now, she took down another bowl and filled it. Then she cut up a salad for her unexpected guest.

"Thanks, Molly. Now I'll have to take you to the meeting just to pay you back." He smiled again.

She thought about dumping the stew in his lap, but she didn't. Instead she gritted her teeth and said nothing.

"Mommy made cupcakes," Sara whispered. "If you eat your stew, you can have one." Then she giggled, pleasure all over her face.

Kaitlin, Sara and Quinn chatted through the rest of the meal, but Molly sat in silence. Only Sara's request for her cupcake drew Molly from her determined withdrawal.

"Yes, sweetie, you did a good job on your stew. You can have your cupcake now."

"Me, too?" Quinn asked, holding up his bowl as Sara had. His behavior drew a giggle from Sara, but not Molly.

She got up and put some cupcakes on a plate and

set them in the center of the table. Then she gave Kaitlin, Sara and Quinn each a saucer.

"Aren't you having any?" Quinn asked.

"No. I want to get the dishes cleaned before I—we leave."

"I'll do the dishes after you've gone," Kaitlin said. "Come have a cupcake."

Molly managed a smile but shook her head.

"I think you should. You may need the extra energy some sugar would give you," Quinn said.

For the first time, Molly realized Quinn might have had another reason for coming.

"Why? What's wrong?"

# Chapter Fourteen

Damn. He hadn't meant to worry her. But he'd heard that Ursula was out persuading any influential person she knew to come tonight to be a roadblock to Molly's success. He'd decided to do a little persuading of his own.

He'd also decided it wouldn't hurt to use his family name for Molly, too. That was why he was escorting her. And why he'd persuaded his father and brothers to be in attendance.

"Ursula's not going down without a fight. I think you should be prepared," he said.

Molly fell back into the chair she'd occupied during dinner. "Do we have a chance?" she asked, her lips trembling.

He wanted to pull her into his arms and warm those lips. So much so that he forgot her question. "Um, what?" he asked, his voice hoarse.

"I asked, do we have a chance?" she repeated, leaning forward.

"Oh, yeah," he replied, then cleared his throat. "We're going to win, Molly, I promise, but it may take a little effort. I've tried to make sure you've got a lot of support tonight, to counterbalance Ursula's crowd.''

Her amazing blue eyes filled with tears. "That's very kind of you."

He nodded. "Amanda will be there, of course, and will speak for you. She's the best, so don't worry."

Sara slipped out of her chair and ran around the table to her mother's side. "I'll help, Mommy. Don't cry."

Molly hugged her little girl. "I'm not crying, sweetie, and you always help me. You're the best."

"So are you," Kaitlin said fiercely. "If that woman—"

Quinn pasted on a smile. "Everything's going to be all right, ladies, I promise." He hoped he was right. Who knew what Ursula Wilson would have come up with?

At least Molly was acting more friendly now. It wouldn't help for him to escort her if she wasn't speaking to him.

"Eat a cupcake, sweetheart, and then we'll—" He realized his mistake at once. So much for friendliness.

"Don't call me that!"

"Uh, it was an accident," he hurriedly assured her, hoping the storminess in her gaze would fade.

"Here's a cupcake, Mommy," Sara said, pulling the plate closer to her mother. "Take this one. It's the biggest."

Looking for a new subject to distract Molly, Quinn turned to Sara. "Did your mom tell you you're coming to Christmas dinner at my house?"

Sara's face lit up with excitement. "Really? Will we have a big turkey and everything?"

Quinn wasn't sure what "everything" included, but he determined they would definitely have it. He wanted the day to be perfect for Sara.

Then he looked at Molly. And realized he'd made another mistake. Clearly Molly hadn't wanted Sara to know about the treat in store for her.

Because she'd been planning to cancel, he realized.

Which made him glad he'd told Sara.

"How lovely," Kaitlin said, her gaze traveling back and forth between him and Molly.

Sara ran around the table, back to her seat beside Quinn, still unaware of her mother's displeasure. "Will there be a big tree, too? With lights?"

"Of course there will. You don't have your tree yet?" he asked, looking around the room.

"Mommy said we'll go shopping for our tree Saturday morning. I can't wait! You want to come?"

"I'd love to," Quinn immediately accepted, knowing Molly would retract the invitation if she could.

"Sara!" Molly protested.

"What, Mommy?"

Quinn watched Molly stare at her daughter. It was easy to understand her dilemma. He wasn't Sara's father, but he wanted the best for the little girl. He had a hard time denying her anything. Molly loved Sara more than he did. How could she wipe the sunshine from that beautiful face?

"Mr. Spencer is probably very busy this weekend. He won't have time to— He probably has to go to Chicago to see...someone."

"Nope, I'm free," he assured her, beaming almost as much as Sara.

"We may not be able to go because of the weather."

Quinn shrugged his shoulders. "I'll check with you Saturday morning." He couldn't hold back a grin at the frustration on her face. "Better eat your cupcake. We need to leave soon."

He watched her, concentrating on lips even more enticing than the cupcake, as she followed his suggestion.

THEY DIDN'T HAVE FAR TO GO to the meeting, and Molly kept silent in his car. She needed to put aside her frustration in dealing with this man and concentrate on the meeting.

But it wasn't easy. He found ways around every roadblock she put up. And Sara didn't help matters. She thought Quinn was wonderful.

She sneaked a look at him as he drove. Unfortunately, he *was* wonderful. Unless you wanted him to be a daddy, a family man, a man who stayed for the long haul. Then he was a disaster.

"We're here," Quinn announced as he turned into the parking lot.

She bowed her head. So much for concentrating on the meeting.

When he killed the motor, instead of opening his door, Quinn turned to face her.

"Yes?" she asked, wondering what he was going to say.

"Molly, I know you're upset with me, but it's important that we present a united front. The Spencer name counts for something, and I want everyone to know the Spencers are on your side."

She swallowed and lifted her chin. "I appreciate that."

"So can we put everything aside and act like friends?"

How could she throw his offer back in his face? It was very generous, particularly since he knew she was angry with him.

"Yes. I'm grateful for your support."

He grinned and leaned toward her. "No problem."

Molly opened the door and slid out into the cold before he could come any closer. She feared he intended to kiss her, and her composure would be shattered if that happened.

When she reached the door to the building, he was beside her, holding it open. Inside, she removed her coat and gloves and hung everything on one of the hooks lining the wall. Then she jerked in surprise as Quinn took one of her hands in his.

"Friends, remember?" he whispered in her ear, sending shivers through her body.

"Oh, good, you're here," Amanda Trask called. She was standing at the entrance to the chamber where the meeting would be held. "I've saved some seats down front."

Quinn led her to Amanda's side. "Everything look all right?"

Amanda gave them a calm smile that eased the flutters in Molly's stomach. "There are a lot of people here, even with the storm on its way. It will be a lively meeting. But I think we're prepared." She drew a deep breath, then turned to Molly. "Your job is to look relaxed and happy. Are you prepared to answer questions?"

She nodded, afraid to try to speak. Quinn squeezed

her hand which, in spite of her anger with him, made her feel good. She wasn't standing alone tonight. These two were with her. It was a nice feeling.

Quinn whispered again. "All right, Molly my girl, paste on a smile and let's get this show on the road." Then he led her into the room, still holding her hand.

Amanda was right. There was a crowd. And when she and Quinn appeared, there seemed to be a lot of whispering. Whether that was because of the zoning change or Quinn holding her hand, she didn't know.

The first part of the meeting was boring, with committee reports and administrative things that didn't apply to Molly's business. But Quinn continued to hold her hand, and she focused on the warmth that came from his touch. She lost track of time until Amanda rose and walked to the microphone to speak to the council.

She presented Molly's request for the zoning change as if she had every confidence in the world that it would be accepted.

Then Ursula Wilson went into action.

She had a list of difficulties. When Amanda tried to answer the first on the list, the question of parking, Ursula suggested Molly answer, rather than hide behind a lawyer. There was a smattering of applause for her demand.

Again Amanda exhibited confidence, only it was confidence in Molly, not herself.

A momentary panic kept Molly silent until Quinn squeezed her hand again. With a grateful smile in his direction, she stood and walked over to the mike.

With a smile that she hoped emulated Amanda's confident one, she said, "Certainly, Mrs. Wilson. I'll be glad to respond to your objections."

After she'd explained the provisions she'd made for parking, Ursula wanted to discuss the possibility of noise that might disturb the peace of Ivy Lane, as Quinn had foreseen.

Molly relaxed just a little. "You see, Breakfast Inn Bed is intended to be a romantic retreat, a place where couples can escape the frantic pace of their lives to concentrate on each other." With a wide smile, she added, "Frankly, I don't expect to see a great deal of my guests, nor do I expect them to want a disco in the living room. I believe their pursuits will be...private."

Amusement ran through the audience at her inference.

"Well, how absolutely disgusting!" Ursula exclaimed. "Are you going to guarantee that these people have a marriage license?"

Molly hadn't been prepared for that question, but she answered it honestly. "No more than any other hotel or inn. As long as both guests are of legal age, I don't feel it is my duty to guide their morals."

When Ursula appeared ready to debate the matter, the president of the council requested that she move on and present any other concerns about their ruling.

With a triumphant look, she assured the council she was concerned for the lack of loyalty to one of the most beloved couples in Tyler, the Santoris. She felt it was the duty of the citizens of Tyler to support their own.

Both Amanda and Molly stepped forward to respond to her claim, but before they could speak, Joe Santori stood.

"I believe I would be the best person to respond to Mrs. Wilson's words."

The president of the council nodded, and Joe, with a warm smile for Molly, stepped forward. "Molly's been in Tyler almost a year now, and I feel she's one of us. Even more important, when she first came to town, she visited with us to find out how we'd feel about competition."

He turned and looked at Molly with a big grin. "I don't think most prospective businesses would do that. We appreciated her thoughtfulness. We have to turn down a lot of business because we're a small operation. The Kelseys, who Molly also visited, do, too. It will be nice to have another outlet for the business. Instead of discouraging people from visiting Tyler, Molly's Breakfast Inn Bed will increase the economic opportunities for all the businesses in our city."

There was a lot of applause.

Johnny Kelsey stood and seconded Joe's words.

The knots in Molly's stomach began to ease. Ursula brought up several more complaints, but they were easily dismissed. Then several people, including Elias Spencer, spoke in favor of Molly's business.

Finally Molly's request was approved unanimously.

Afterward, with tears in her eyes, she tried to express gratitude to those who had supported her, saying how much she appreciated being made to feel a part of Tyler.

"We only told the truth," Joe Santori assured her. "But it was Quinn here who called to remind us that we needed to show up. So thank him, too."

Molly smiled tremulously and tried to think of what to say.

"She's already thanked me," Quinn assured everyone with a laugh. "I got another home-cooked meal tonight."

There were several comments about Molly trying to trap Quinn into domesticity. Molly kept a smile on her lips, dismissing their words as if they were a huge joke.

"We really appreciate everyone coming out," Quinn said, interrupting the teasing, "but, with the storm coming, I think we'd all better cut things short. I heard on the radio we may get over a foot of snow."

"Looks like the snow season is starting off with a bang," Joe said. "If you're putting pictures in your brochure, get some while the snow is clean and white, Molly. Makes everything look really romantic."

"Thanks for the advice. I will."

"Thanks again," Quinn called as he took Molly's hand and pulled her after him to the door.

"We'll see you Christmas Day, if not before," Elias said.

Quinn noted Molly's acquiescent smile, feeling sure now she and Sara would come, since Sara was so enthusiastic about the celebration. Molly wouldn't let her personal feelings hurt her child.

After putting on their coats, Quinn pushed open the door to discover that the storm had arrived. The flakes weren't the large, fluttery kind. They were small and spitting at everything in the storm's path. Already the ground was completely white.

Quinn wrapped an arm around Molly and rushed her toward his car. This time she didn't protest the protection he afforded her. She owed him a lot.

Once they were in the vehicle, sheltered from the storm, Quinn started the car but left it in Neutral. "We'd better give it a minute to warm up." She nodded and he ducked his head to see her expression. "Are you relieved?"

She offered him a smile. "Yes, thank you. I realize how much I owe you for your support."

"Enough to let me join you Saturday morning?"

She didn't say anything.

"Molly?"

She looked at him again. "I only wanted to protect Sara. She doesn't understand— What if she— Never mind. Yes, of course, if your idea of fun is to go out in the cold and look at trees, you're welcome to join us. And I'll fix lunch for us, too."

"Lady, that's an offer I'd never refuse." He eased the car into gear and headed for Ivy Lane.

THE STORM WAS STILL RAGING the next morning. Kaity's Kids was closed, much to Sara's chagrin.

"But, Mommy, we could have snowball fights!" Sara complained.

"You can have them when the storm stops."

"Really?"

"Yes. And I have an idea. How about if I call Jeremy's mother and see if he can go with us tomorrow to find our Christmas tree and then have lunch? Would you like that?"

Sara began jumping up and down, clapping for her mother's suggestion. Suddenly she stopped. "But Mr. Spencer will still come, won't he?"

Molly sighed. "Yes, unless something comes up." After a moment, she added, "He's a very busy man, you know, but he's welcome to come."

"Goody. He'll come. He said he would. Let's go call Jeremy now."

Molly complied with Sara's request. She'd had the idea to invite Jeremy to divert Sara from focusing totally on Quinn. She was doing all she could to protect her daughter.

Pam was delighted with the invitation. "Thanks so much. This will give me time to finish up my Santa shopping. Can I take Sara another day and let you do the same?"

"That's not necessary, Pam. I've finished my shopping. But having Jeremy with us will make it so much more fun when we find our tree."

"Great. What time should I bring him over?"

"We'll pick him up about ten o'clock, if that's okay, but I'll let you come get him Saturday afternoon after they've played."

"You've got a deal and a great big thank-you."

Molly hung up the phone with a sigh. She could put her conscience aside tomorrow, knowing she'd done her best for Sara. And she could be grateful for Quinn's muscles. Two years ago, just before Christopher's death, she'd gone out to get a tree by herself. Christopher was too busy to waste his time on anything for his family.

Molly's eyes had chosen a tree she could barely carry. She could admit to relief that Quinn would deal with the tree tomorrow. The big old Victorian home cried out for a big tree.

Which reminded her that she needed to drag out the box of decorations and see what supplies she'd need to purchase tomorrow.

She hurried up the stairs to the storage room on the third floor.

As she did so, she remembered she needed to figure out what she'd be serving for lunch tomorrow. And she wanted to make some Christmas cookies and some fudge. As usual, she had too much to do. But at least all the activity would prevent any thoughts of one Quinn Spencer.

"MOMMY, I'M READY," Sara announced, running into the kitchen.

Molly couldn't help smiling. Since she'd accepted Quinn's presence today, she'd found herself getting more excited, too. She loved all the trappings of the Christmas season.

"Good."

"Is it time to go get Jeremy?"

"I forgot to tell you. Mr. Spencer is picking up Jeremy on his way here. We're going to use his car because it's bigger." Quinn had a Jeep Cherokee that would make it easier to bring a tree home.

"I'll go watch for them!" Sara said, and raced out of the kitchen again.

Molly took the last pan of cookies out of the oven. She'd been up since six, baking Christmas tree, bell and candy cane cookies. She even had all but the last two batches decorated. Homemade tomato soup was gently bubbling on the back burner, and she had a tuna casserole in the refrigerator that could be heated while they ate soup.

The snow had stopped, but it was very cold. They'd need something hot when they got home.

"They're here! They're here!" Sara screamed from the front of the house.

Molly turned off the oven and wiped her hands.

Drawing a deep breath, she headed for the front of the house to greet their guests.

Sara was putting on her coat already.

"Don't forget your gloves and hat. It's very cold," Molly warned. She'd put her outerwear on the desk by the stairs. As she slipped into her coat, she heard Quinn sound his horn. She'd told him they'd come out when the two males of their party arrived.

"Come on, Mommy!" Sara called, tugging on the front door.

"I'm right behind you, sweetie, but don't run on the snow. You might fall."

When they reached the car, Molly discovered Jeremy was as excited as Sara. Slipping into the front seat, Molly leaned toward Quinn and asked, "Was he bouncing off the ceiling all the way over here?"

He grinned. "Yeah. How about Sara?"

Molly nodded. "She wasn't even interested longer than five minutes in making Christmas cookies."

"Christmas cookies?" Quinn asked.

"I should've known food would catch your attention," she said with an exasperated smile.

Quinn's face sobered. "I never had a mother who did special things like that. I think Sara's a lucky little girl."

Molly felt compassion squeeze her heart. She couldn't hold back a soft smile. "Thank you. I'm lucky to have Sara. She's—she's special."

"So she is, but that's not surprising. Her mother's pretty special, too."

## Chapter Fifteen

Their first stop was to purchase new lights, some garlands, and a new ornament for each of the children. Quinn made a secret purchase, too. He found a glass ornament in the shape of a Victorian house resembling Molly's.

He couldn't resist.

When they reached the Christmas tree lot, the shopping was as much fun but a lot colder. The two children ran back and forth among the trees, choosing first one and then another.

Quinn followed Molly as she slowly studied each tree, giving it her entire concentration. He smiled as he watched, loving the way she threw her heart into every project. When she found the tree she wanted, an eight-foot Douglas fir, he immediately seconded her choice.

"Are you sure it won't be too big for us to manage?" she asked him.

He wanted to tell her he'd tackle a tree twice that big if it would please her. Bringing that sweet smile to Molly's face was a never-ending goal for him. But he knew she'd back away if he said those things. So he simply assured her they could manage the big tree.

When they reached the house, the tree strapped to the roof of his vehicle, he and Molly carried the tree to the front porch.

"You do have a stand, don't you?" he asked.

"Yes. I found one in the attic. I'll go get it." She started to enter the house, then remembered the kids. "Sara, you and Jeremy put our packages in the living room. Then take off your coats and wash your hands for lunch."

"No! I want to decorate the tree first!" Sara demanded, excitement still on her face.

Quinn turned to Molly, wondering what her response would be. As much as he loved Sara, he didn't want her acting like a brat.

"Sara, please do as I ask and mind your manners, or you won't get to help decorate the tree." Molly's voice was firm but not angry, and it affected Sara at once. Her eyes looked like big blue saucers and she gasped. Then she became subdued.

"Yes, Mommy," she muttered, and hurried into the house, Jeremy right behind her.

"I'm sorry. Sometimes excitement makes her forget her manners," Molly apologized.

"I'm sure that's true for most kids. But you handle her well. How do you always know what to do?"

She gave him a wry smile. "I don't. But I love her…and I pay attention to what she says. And then I wing it," she added, "and hope I'm doing the right thing."

"Well, you've got my vote."

"Thanks. I'll get the tree stand."

Quinn shook the tree to remove any snow still clinging to its branches, but he thought about Molly's explanation about parenting. One of his reasons for choosing not to have children was the fear of making mistakes.

With Molly's rule as a guideline, he thought parenting might be possible. But it was so easy to make mistakes. Like his mother. Maybe she hadn't intended to harm her children, but she had.

"Here it is," Molly said, coming back out onto the porch.

As he worked to put the tree in its stand, she said, "Oh, did I tell you that the open house paid off for my bed and breakfast? I've already got three suites booked for Valentine's Day weekend."

He was pleased his idea had helped her. "Anyone I know?"

"Mmm, I don't think I should give out that information. But I think it will be interesting. One suite is for honeymooners. The other two are…intriguing."

He raised an eyebrow as he tightened the screws in the base of the tree. "Ah. Well, keep me posted."

By that time, he had the big tree in the stand, and he carried it into the living room.

"We want it in the window so everyone can see our lights," Sara said, obviously having recovered from her admonishment a few minutes ago.

"Yes, I think you're right, Sara," Molly agreed. "Is there room, Quinn?"

He added respect to Molly's brand of parenting. She gave Sara respect, considering her requests. It didn't mean she always gave in, but she considered her daughter's opinion.

"Yes, there's room." He set the tree in place and stood back. "How does it look?"

"Perfect," Molly said, smiling at him.

He felt as if he'd climbed Mt. Everest because he'd pleased Molly.

"Mommy, can't we—" Sara was about to ask again to decorate the tree, but one look from her mother and she left the thought unspoken.

"Time for lunch so we'll thaw out," Molly said, and herded all of them to the kitchen.

Lunch was delicious, as usual. Not only was the food tasty, but also there was a warmth of emotion, a camaraderie that Quinn had seldom felt before. There had been a few times with his father and brothers, but they had lacked the sweetness that Molly brought to life.

When lunch had been consumed, Molly suggested they wait until they'd trimmed the tree to have Christmas cookies. Her suggestion got an enthusiastic approval from the children.

For the next hour the four of them decorated the tree. First the lights went up, Quinn handling the actual placement and Molly directing, with a lot of help from Sara and Jeremy.

Then, using a stepladder, Quinn placed the star on the very top of the tree. The garlands were added. As the two children hung their special ornaments, Quinn handed his sack to Molly.

"What's this?" she asked, a puzzled look on her face.

"A special ornament for you."

Sara, having already hung the Santa Claus ornament she'd chosen, rushed to her mother's side. Jeremy followed her.

"What is it?" Sara asked.

Molly reached in the bag and pulled out a delicate glass ornament in the shape of a Victorian house.

Quinn found himself holding his breath for her reaction. He'd given other women gifts, more expensive gifts, but their reactions had never mattered as much as Molly's.

"Oh, Quinn," she whispered, awe in her voice. "It's beautiful! I didn't see this one at the store. Thank you so much! It looks like our house. See, Sara?"

"It's beautiful," Sara agreed. "Want me to hang it for you?"

"Thank you, sweetie, but I think I'll hang this one myself."

The smile she sent Quinn was almost as good as kissing her, he decided. As he remembered their embrace, he changed his mind. The smile was wonderful, but not quite that good. He wondered if he'd ever have the opportunity to hold her and kiss her again.

She carefully placed the ornament high on the tree so that it would be protected from accidents. Then she opened the boxes of other ornaments and began handing the round colored balls to Jeremy and Sara.

"I think we'll need to hang some of these, too," she said to Quinn. "Otherwise, the tree will only be decorated the first four feet."

With a smile, he joined in hanging the decorations.

As they neared the end, Molly disappeared for a few minutes. She came back in with a tray just as they deemed the tree complete.

A big tray of cookies and fudge, surrounded by four cups, drew everyone's attention. "I have hot chocolate for Jeremy and Sara, and coffee for the two of us," she told Quinn.

With the Christmas tree lights on, the four of them

sat down and admired their handiwork while they enjoyed their dessert.

"This is the bestest day ever," Sara said as she munched on a cookie.

"You're right," Molly said, "but don't speak until you've finished chewing."

"My mom says that to me, too," Jeremy said.

"Jeremy, remind me when it's time to go home and I'll get your ornament for you. It looks beautiful on our tree, but you can take it home and put it on your tree if you want."

Much to Quinn's surprise, Jeremy refused. "I have lots of ornaments on my tree, and I like sharing my ornament with Sara," Jeremy said, smiling at his best friend.

Sara leaned over and hugged Jeremy's neck before picking up another cookie.

Quinn understood what Jeremy meant. He liked knowing that something he'd given them would always be a part of Christmas for Molly and Sara.

"He's going to be a heartbreaker when he grows up," Molly whispered to Quinn.

Before he could answer, Sara jumped up and ran around the coffee table to hug Quinn's neck.

He hugged her back, of course, but then he asked, "What was that for?"

"I'm glad you came today. It's like you're my real daddy," Sara said, beaming up at him.

Quinn froze as panic riddled his heart.

"HEY, IT'S SATURDAY NIGHT!" Brady exclaimed as he came in the back door of Elias's house to find Quinn sitting at the kitchen table, staring glumly at the cup of coffee in front of him.

Quinn looked up and stared at his brother. "So?"

"Your playboy image is going to disappear if you hang around the house every weekend."

Quinn gave his brother a disgusted look and took a sip of coffee.

"Where's Dad?"

"Out" was Quinn's only response.

Brady grabbed a mug and poured himself some coffee, then joined Quinn at the table. "Let me guess. Lydia?"

Quinn nodded.

The back door opened again and Seth stomped into the kitchen, unbuttoning his coat. "Hi. Where's Dad?"

Quinn rolled his eyes and said nothing.

Brady replied, "Out with Lydia. Where's Jenna?"

"Already tucked up in bed. This pregnancy is tiring her out. I told her I'd ask Dad about Christmas dinner, for her to go on to sleep." Seth got his own cup of coffee and joined his brothers.

"Man, it's pretty pitiful when Dad has more social life than any of us," Brady complained.

Quinn said, without looking up from his mug, "Maybe it's about time he enjoys life."

"Yeah," Brady agreed. "But what about us?"

"I don't know about you two," Seth said with a smile, "but in case you hadn't noticed, I have a wife and a baby on the way."

Quinn looked at his older brother. "Are you scared?"

"Hell, yes, I'm scared. Babies are a big responsibility," Seth said. "But I sure couldn't face the alternative, life without Jenna. And I damn sure wasn't going to make the mistake our mother did and abandon any child I've made.''

No one said anything for a while.

Finally Brady changed the subject. "You both going to the Christmas Eve bash?"

Seth and Quinn nodded.

"You taking Molly?" Brady asked Quinn.

Quinn shook his head no. He wanted to, but he couldn't. Sara's words had erected a big stop sign. He never intended to risk harming a child, as his mother had harmed him and his brothers.

"Why not?"

Seth chimed in. "Don't tell me you're bringing Clarisse. If you are, we won't be sharing a table with you."

"Clarisse isn't that bad," Quinn protested, but without any heart.

Brady gave a derisive snort. "She's no Cinderella, either."

"I'm coming alone."

"Then I guess I'll be your date," Brady said with a grin. "I haven't asked anyone, either."

"Man, you two are going to make the family look bad. What's the matter with you? Quinn, why aren't you bringing Molly?"

"Because I don't want to get involved. She has a kid!" He took a deep breath to calm himself. After a sip of coffee, he added, "I'm not interested in family life."

More silence.

Then Seth said, "Mom really did a number on us, didn't she? I'm grateful Jenna forced me to wake up and smell the coffee."

Quinn asked abruptly, "Has Cooper found out anything yet about our half sibling?"

"Not yet. He's got a couple of leads he's following," Seth said.

"Good. I think it's time we settled our past. Running away from what happened to us as kids sure isn't helping anything."

"Anything being Molly?" Brady asked softly.

Quinn closed his eyes momentarily, then squared his shoulders and stared at Brady. "Molly's a friend. Nothing else. I'm not interested in settling down. I like to pick up and go when I feel like it."

"Like tonight?" Brady asked, grinning.

Quinn gave him a disgusted look and turned to Seth. "Why don't you call Coop and anyone else you can think of and let's play poker. I might as well increase my wealth if I'm going to be here tonight." Besides, it might take his mind off the day he'd spent with Molly and Sara.

Brady laughed. "Yeah, like you can take us! I could use some of your money to buy a new portable X-ray machine for my office, though. I'm game."

"You two are wishful thinkers. I need to buy new baby shoes. So I reckon I'll have the advantage," he assured them with a laugh as he headed for the phone on the wall.

Quinn didn't really care who won. He just wanted something to occupy his mind other than Molly, and the sweet smile she'd given him when she'd hung the glass house on the tree. Or the joy in Sara's eyes as she'd told him he was acting like her daddy.

Losing money would be better than thinking about those things.

MONDAY EVENING, after tucking Sara in bed, Molly returned to the kitchen. But she had nothing to cook or clean. She didn't even have anything to plan. The rest of the evening spread out before her, as empty as could be.

For the first time in ages she had time on her hands. Time to think about the future. The empty future.

She'd known she'd already gone too far in time spent with Quinn. She'd actually fallen in love with the difficult, sexy man. But she hoped she'd save Sara from the pain *she* was feeling.

Because she'd known, as soon as Sara had mentioned the word *daddy* to Quinn, that any secret hope she'd had that Quinn would come to love her and Sara was pointless.

He'd managed to depart about two minutes after Sara had mentioned that dreaded word. With good manners, of course. But he'd gone.

After Jeremy had gone home, she'd sat down with Sara and had a discussion.

She'd begun with something Sara would understand. "You love Jeremy as a friend, don't you, Sara?"

"Yes, he's the bestest friend in the whole, wide world!" she'd exclaimed with her usual enthusiasm.

"And you love Mr. Spencer, too, don't you?"

"Oh, yes, Mommy!"

"But Jeremy's not your brother, is he?"

"No, but I wish he was."

"Okay. And Mr. Spencer is not your daddy, is he?"

Sara repeated herself. "No, but I wish he was."

"Wishing is okay, sweetheart, but it won't come

true. Jeremy will always be your friend, not your brother. And Mr. Spencer will—will be a friend, too, but not your daddy.''

''But, Mommy, Jeremy already has a mommy and daddy. But Mr. Spencer doesn't got a little girl. Why can't he—''

''Because he can't,'' Molly had said firmly.

''But then we can't be a patchwork family, like you said,'' Sara complained, a sad look on her face.

''No, we can't, Sara. But it's important to be grateful that we have each other. We're pretty lucky, aren't we?'' she asked, smiling with all the love in her heart for her child.

''Yeah, we're lucky, Mommy. But it's okay to *wish* Mr. Spencer could be my daddy, right?''

''As long as you understand it won't happen.''

Molly sat at the kitchen table, thinking about the past few days after her discussion with Sara. Her little girl seemed all right, but several times she'd caught Sara in the living room, the tree lights on, sitting below the tree, staring up and whispering.

When Molly asked her who she was talking to, she'd hurriedly said, ''No one,'' and asked her mother for a snack.

The phone rang, dragging Molly from her thoughts.

''Hi, it's Pam. I have an idea.''

''About what?''

''Did you get your invitation to the Christmas Eve party this Sunday night at the Timberlake Lodge?''

Molly knew exactly what Pam was talking about. Each year the Chamber of Commerce held a huge party at the Timberlake Lodge, the most exclusive place in Tyler, well, actually, outside Tyler. All the movers and shakers attended.

All local businesspeople received an invitation. Molly had gotten hers last week, but she'd put it away, knowing she wouldn't be attending. She wasn't going to leave her daughter alone on Christmas Eve.

"Yes, I got it, but I'm not going," she told Pam.

"Why not?"

"Sara and I are going to wait for Santa together." She tried to add a chuckle afterward, but she wasn't sure it came out right. She hadn't been in a laughing mood since Saturday.

"Here's my idea. Grandma Martha takes Jeremy each Christmas Eve. He spends the night with her at Worthington House. They play games and read stories and he eats way too much candy. Then she tucks him in. We pick him up the next morning after Santa has come, and we come to the house and open presents. It's Jeremy's favorite thing, and he's spoiled rotten by Martha and her friends."

"How nice of Martha. Her energy is amazing, isn't it?" Molly had no idea where Pam was going with her story, but she wasn't listening closely. She had too much on her mind.

"Yes. But this year, Jeremy wants Sara to come with him."

Molly realized she should've paid better attention. "Oh, no! That's too much for Martha. I wouldn't want—"

"I've already talked to Martha. She thinks it's a great idea. It will be even more fun for Jeremy to have Sara there. He considers her to be his sister."

"I know they're close, but she shouldn't horn in on his family traditions."

After a silence, Pam said, her voice serious, "You know, I worry about Jeremy being an only child. But since you moved to town, he doesn't feel that way. I think he's adopted Sara. And it's made him a better person, to have someone besides himself to consider."

Molly remembered the child's response about the ornament.

"He's a wonderful boy, and his friendship is important to Sara."

"So let her come with him. In the morning, you can pick her up and have Christmas. I heard you're going to the Spencers for Christmas dinner."

If Quinn didn't call to tell her to stay home. Which was a possibility.

"All right. If you're sure it won't be too much for Martha."

"She's looking forward to it. So Patrick and I will pick you both up at six-thirty. Martha would like us to come in and show the ladies our fancy dresses. What will you wear?"

"I wasn't planning on going. I think maybe I should stay home."

"Don't you dare. The more people you talk to, the more likely they'll be to remember your business when they have visitors coming to town. Or mention it to friends who express a desire to get away. You can even write off the cost of your gown for taxes."

But Quinn would be there.

Suddenly she straightened and drew in a deep breath. If Quinn couldn't love her and Sara, it was his problem, not hers. She wasn't going to skulk in the shadows of life because he was too stupid to know what was good for him.

"You're right, Pam. How dressy do they get at this thing?"

"*Very* dressy. The sky's the limit."

"Does Gates Department Store carry anything that will work?"

"Oh, yes, and they keep track of what everyone's bought. They won't sell you a duplicate. I'm so glad you're going! We'll have so much fun."

"Thanks for asking me, Pam. You're a terrific friend."

After Molly hung up the phone, she sagged in her chair. The moment of determination had faded, and she wondered if she'd made a mistake. Then she straightened her shoulders again. No, she hadn't. She was part of the community to stay, whether Quinn Spencer was here or not.

She'd survived the past. She'd survive the future.

With her chin in the air. And the best darn dress Gates Department Store had to offer on her back.

She'd show Quinn Spencer.

# Chapter Sixteen

Quinn's head was no clearer a week later than it had been the night after he'd helped decorate Molly's tree.

He kept his distance from the charming house on Ivy Lane, and its tempting occupants. They'd stayed in his head, of course. He'd even bought several presents for Sara to go under his father's tree.

He'd bought nothing for Molly.

How could he? He seemed on the verge of something and one false move would throw him over the edge. He didn't know what would await him, and he was afraid to find out.

He told himself he wanted Molly. In his bed.

But that was all.

He knew he was doing what he'd done all his adult life: He was retreating from commitment.

He yanked the tie he'd just tied to start again. What was wrong with him? He could tie a tuxedo tie in his sleep. It was almost time to leave for the Christmas Eve party and he wanted to get there so he could come home at a decent hour.

"Concentrate, Spencer!" he snapped to himself.

All week long, that had been his problem. Fortunately, no one expected much work to be accomplished the week before Christmas.

The real problem was he was at war. His heart wanted Molly in every way. But his brain kept telling him he had no business taking her and Sara into his life. He wasn't husband or parent material. He might actually take after his mother. He might walk away.

How could he do that to Molly and Sara?

"Damn!" he muttered, and started doing his tie again.

When he finally reached the Timberlake Lodge, he sat in his car for several minutes. Elegantly dressed couples were entering the massive building, its history as a hunting lodge in sharp contrast to the long gowns and tuxedos. But even before Eddie Wocheck came home to Tyler to purchase the lodge as part of his hotel chain, the place had been the center of social life in Tyler.

Judson Ingalls, the previous owner, now way past the age of retirement, had done a lot of entertaining. Quinn knew he and his wife Tisha, owner of The Hair Affair, would be inside, greeting all arrivals, as if they still lived in the majestic building.

With a sigh, he got out of the car and headed for the front door, hoping to slip in unobtrusively.

Fat chance. He laughed silently at his unreal hopes. He was greeted, as he'd known, by Judson and Tisha. They were amazingly active for their ages. Even Tisha's heart attack a few years ago hadn't slowed her down. It was Tisha, always forthright, who noted his lack of a date.

"Quinn Spencer, what are you doing here by yourself? Don't tell me you couldn't find a date!"

"I was too tired to look for one, Tisha. Amanda's working me too hard."

"Probably because of her baby. Well, don't worry. We'll be on the lookout for a lady for you."

He silently groaned but moved on to greet the Wochecks. Eddie's wife was Alyssa Ingalls Baron Wocheck, Judson's daughter. When Eddie had come back to Tyler, he'd discovered his old love, Alyssa, was alone, and he'd promptly married her. Her daughter was Amanda, Quinn's partner.

Though Alyssa raised an eyebrow when she realized he was alone, she only said, "Your brother was across the room talking to Jeff the last I saw. Since Brady's alone, too, I suppose you can hang out together. Though why two eligible bachelors like you don't have women all around you, I don't know."

Since Jeff was a doctor at Tyler General, as well as being Alyssa's son and Amanda's brother, Quinn wasn't surprised. He and Brady worked together.

"Thanks," he said to Alyssa with a smile. "I'll head in that direction."

"Don't forget to dance with all the single ladies."

"Darn it," he told Alyssa with a grin, "I was planning on dancing with Cece."

Alyssa grinned. "You can try, but Jeff's pretty protective."

Cece, Jeff's wife, was an old friend because she was the nursing supervisor of Worthington House, providing care for his favorite ladies.

A sudden protest rose in him at that description. Of course Martha and her cohorts were his favorite ladies, he assured himself, but he knew there was a part of him he hadn't convinced.

He suddenly wished he'd invited Molly to come

to the party with him. He'd thought about it, but with the rumors already spreading from the meeting when they held hands, he knew better.

"Hey, Quinn," a man called, and he turned around to see Johnny and Anna Kelsey.

"Hi, Johnny, Anna."

"Good job the other night. You and Amanda had your bases covered."

Anna leaned closer. "Where's Molly?"

Quinn pretended to survey the crowd. "I don't know. I haven't seen her. Is she here?" He was pretty sure she wouldn't be. It would mean leaving Sara alone on Christmas Eve.

Anna looked shocked. "I thought— I mean, we just got here. I'll keep an eye out for her."

Quinn excused himself and continued on just as the orchestra began to play.

Couples took the floor, gracefully moving to the strains of a waltz.

He caught the eye of Brick Bauer and his wife, Karen, on the dance floor, both members of local police forces. He'd had a juvenile run-in or two with Brick, but they'd become friends as Quinn matured. The man waved to him, and motioned for him to join the dancers.

Again Quinn silently cursed himself for coming alone. He shook his head to Brick and walked a little faster, looking for Brady across the room.

Instead of Brady, he saw his father, with Lydia at his side, talking to someone. It surprised him to see it was Caroline, the waitress from Marge's Diner, chatting with his father. He was glad to see she was all right after that near-disaster with the hot coffee at the diner. But something about that incident still bothered him.

He pushed it aside as he walked passed the Santoris, including Gina. He didn't recognize her escort, which didn't surprise him. The only man she'd ever been serious about was K. J. Eber, a popular cartoonist who'd left Tyler after their breakup a few years ago. At least she hadn't come alone. He wished he'd been as smart.

Having reached the other side of the room, he scanned the sidelines, looking for his brother. But he couldn't see him anywhere.

"You looking for Molly Blake?" Nora Gates Forrester asked, touching his arm. She and her husband, Byron, were chatting with another couple nearby.

"Molly? Is she here?" Quinn asked, then regretted his words.

"Of course she is, and wearing one of my favorite gowns from the store," Nora replied. She didn't have to say what store. She was the owner of Gates Department Store, inherited from her Aunt Ellie. But she'd expanded and updated the store into a total success.

"Actually, I was looking for Brady," he said stiffly, refusing to look for Molly.

"Then you can kill two birds with one stone," Byron said, waved his hand toward the dance floor. "She's dancing with Brady."

Quinn spun around, his hands going to his hips. What the hell was going on?

Almost as if he'd called their names, Brady and Molly swept by him. Brady was in a tux, of course, but Molly was in an ice-blue satin gown, cut low in front, its small straps almost off her shoulders, the skirt flowing as she gracefully danced by.

"Isn't she lovely?" Nora whispered.

"Uh, yeah. Lovely."

He forgot to thank Nora and Byron for their assistance. Instead, his gaze remained fastened on Brady and Molly. He didn't want to lose track of them.

When the music ended, he'd positioned himself to greet his brother and Molly as they came off the dance floor. "Good evening," he said, trying to sound friendly, but his voice was tight.

"Hey, bro, you made it," Brady said, grinning.

"Yeah, I'm here. May I have the next dance, Molly?"

Before she could answer, the music started again, and he wrapped his arm around her waist and stepped onto the dance floor.

"I didn't say yes," she muttered, her head down.

"Why not? Aren't I as eligible as Brady?"

She jerked her head up. "What does that mean?"

"As a partner. I meant as a dance partner." His heart was beating double time, but he didn't know if it was because of the conversation or because he was finally holding Molly's body against his again.

She sighed and he felt the breath move through her.

"You're holding me too close," she whispered.

He knew he was. He lessened the tension in his arms a fraction, to make her think he was giving her space. Then he whirled her around in a spin and tucked her against him again.

"Where's Sara?"

"She's with Martha for the night."

He looked down at her and realized the view was incredible. The scoop neck of her gown provided a picture frame for her breasts, soft, caressable mounds of flesh.

"Your gown is, uh, lovely, but a little low-cut, don't you think?" All he could think about was other men seeing her like that when she danced with them. Damn it, his own brother was one of them.

She almost stopped moving. "I beg your pardon? After that Clarisse woman's dress, you can call this low-cut?" she asked, outrage in her voice.

She had a point. And he could hardly tell her that Clarisse didn't matter, but Molly did. He'd be over the edge of the cliff with that remark.

He cleared his throat. "I was concerned that some man might respond in an inappropriate manner."

With sarcasm, Molly muttered, "Right, my charms would drive him over the edge. Please, Quinn!"

Her phrasing only underlined his difficulty.

"Did you drive yourself? It might snow again this evening."

"I came with Patrick and Pam. I'm sure he's capable of getting us home. I'll be fine."

He breathed a sigh of relief to know she hadn't come with a date. Someone who would have the right to hold her, to kiss her, to fall madly in love with her like he— No. He was attracted to her. That was all.

The music ended. Which meant he had to release her.

Stepping back, forcing his arms to let her go, he asked, "Want something to eat or drink? We could—"

"I'd better see what Patrick and Pam are doing."
She turned to walk away.

He followed.

"I see you found Molly," Nora said. "But where's Brady?"

Since he'd told Nora and Byron that it was Brady he was looking for, not Molly, Quinn was at a loss for words. "Um, I—"

"I think he was dancing with Eden," Molly said with a smile.

"I don't think we've been introduced," Nora said, but fortunately, she didn't wait for Quinn do to the honors. "I'm Nora Forrester, owner of Gates Department Store. You chose my favorite gown from the store and it looks wonderful on you."

"Oh, thank you. I enjoy shopping there so much. Not only is the merchandise top quality, but you also have the best sales staff in the world."

Nora was pleased with Molly's remarks and introduced her husband. But Quinn didn't want to discuss business in Tyler. And he wasn't terribly interested in sharing Molly with anyone.

He caught Byron watching him, a knowing look in his gaze, and actually felt his cheeks redden. Before he could find a way to end the conversation, however, Byron interrupted his wife. "Dear, I think Quinn and Molly were looking for someone. Maybe we can visit later."

"Oh, yes, of course," Nora agreed, slipping her hand into her husband's and smiling at Molly.

"Come have a cup of coffee with me some morning," Molly said. "I'll show you Breakfast Inn Bed."

"She's a terrific muffin-maker," Quinn added, but

he put his hand around Molly's waist and urged her toward Patrick and Pam standing nearby.

As soon as they left the Forresters, Molly stepped out of his hold and turned to face him. "Don't feel obligated to escort me. I can manage."

"I was just being friendly. We are friends, aren't we?"

She stared up at him, her blue eyes spectacular with the ice-blue of her gown. "No," she said, drawing out the word, "I don't think we are. You finally understood my concerns about you and Sara last Saturday, didn't you? Little girls love the idea of a daddy. I don't want Sara hurt, so I think our…whatever we have is over. Thank you for your legal help. I'll take my difficulties to Amanda from now on."

"What about tomorrow? You are coming tomorrow, aren't you?"

She blushed. "We're coming tomorrow because I don't want to disappoint Sara, but I'd appreciate it if you wouldn't be so nice to her."

Without waiting for an answer, she left him standing there, in shock. She was ending their friendship? She wanted him to stay away? To not be nice to Sara?

He stared after her, suddenly remembering Seth's remarks a week ago. He couldn't bear the alternative of letting Jenna walk out of his life.

Could *he?* Could he forget Molly and Sara? Could he never sit in Molly's warm kitchen, sharing with her and Sara, making plans for the future with the two most important females in the world? Could he cut himself off entirely from that warmth, from those smiles? Could he trust fate to protect the two of them from the evil in the world?

He had no answers, but his head was starting to ache.

"She's a pretty lady," Brick Bauer whispered in Quinn's ear.

He spun around, staring at his old friend. "Yeah."

"A lot of the men around here are looking. You staking a claim?"

Another question he couldn't answer. "You know I'm not the marrying kind," he muttered, shifting his gaze back to Molly, who had rejoined Patrick and Pam.

Brick laughed. "None of us males is the marrying kind," he assured Quinn with a laugh, "until some angel comes along and convinces us we can change."

Quinn turned back to stare at Brick. "Do you think we can change?"

"Look at your brother Seth. He was as gun-shy of marriage as you and Brady. Now he's happily married, if that permanent grin is any indication, and has a baby on the way. That's a pretty big change."

"Yeah," Quinn agreed, but his gaze returned to Molly.

For the next hour, Quinn stood around, visiting with old friends and keeping an eye on Molly. He hardly noticed the looks he drew. He didn't care if everyone realized he was watching her. Someone had to look out for her.

Finally he approached her and asked for another dance.

After a quick look at him, she looked down at her

hands, twisted in front of her and declined. "I'm rather tired, actually."

"Want to go home? I'll be glad to give you a ride."

"Are you leaving soon?"

He wanted to tell her he'd leave whenever if she went with him. He wasn't exactly having a wonderful evening, watching other men hold her. Instead, he simply said, "Yeah."

He could see a struggle in her eyes, but she finally said, "If you don't mind, I'd appreciate a ride when you're ready to go."

"We'd better go tell Pam, then." He wasn't going to give her time to change her mind.

"If you're sure," Pam said. "If you want to wait about half an hour, we'll be ready to leave then." Pam looked at Quinn as if she questioned his motives.

"Quinn's leaving now, and I'm really tired. I've been painting late into the night, so I need my sleep."

"Okay," Pam agreed with a smile.

"I'll go warm up the car and pick you up at the front door," Quinn murmured, hoping to escape before Molly changed her mind.

"Do you want me to pick up Sara in the morning and drop her off when I get Jeremy?" Pam asked after she watched Quinn walk away.

"Would you mind? I've got some cooking to do before we go to the Spencers' tomorrow."

"Nope, I'll be glad to. Just...be careful," Pam said, squeezing Molly's hand.

"Yes, of course," Molly agreed, not sure what

Pam meant. Then she hurried to get her wrap before joining Quinn.

She'd discovered Pam was right about the benefits of attending the party. But she was weary. Life didn't have the sparkle it had had when she moved to Tyler, with a clear plan in her head and enthusiasm in her heart.

"You're being foolish," she muttered to herself as she approached the door and Quinn. She knew the problem. And she would get over it. As soon as she put some distance between herself and Quinn Spencer.

*And so you're going home with him now?*

Not with him! She was accepting a ride, that was all. With a full day tomorrow, she needed to get some rest.

But rest wasn't what consumed her when she slid into Quinn's Jeep Cherokee.

After several minutes of no conversation, Quinn asked, "So, you've been doing some painting?"

"Yes, getting the other suites ready for when the quilts are delivered. I'm opening on February fourteenth, you know, so I don't have much time left. I told you I already have three bookings," she told him, trying to sound enthusiastic.

"Terrific. Maybe you should hire someone to finish the painting. You don't want to wear yourself out."

"No, I can do it myself."

Since Timberlake Lodge was only twenty minutes from Tyler, they didn't discuss much else until he turned onto Ivy Lane.

"What time are you coming tomorrow?" he asked.

"Your father said to come around noon," she reminded him.

"You can come earlier, if you want." He watched her out of the corner of his eye.

She shook her head. "I have some baking to do before we come."

He pulled into the driveway. "How's the tree?"

"Beautiful. We appreciate your help."

"Mind if I come in and look at it again?"

Molly didn't know what to say. She didn't think it would be a good idea to be alone with Quinn, but they wouldn't have managed the tree without him. It seemed inhospitable to refuse his request. Finally she said, "Of course not."

He killed the motor and got out of the car and came around it to open her door. Because she had to gather her full skirt before she got out, she hadn't made much progress before he was beside her.

"Is that wrap warm enough?" he asked.

She'd simply taken a black pashmina, a wool shawl-like cape that had been popular for a while, and used it for tonight. She didn't want to spend a lot of money on an evening coat that she would seldom use. "It's fine."

As if he didn't believe her, he wrapped his arm around her shoulders and hurried her to the porch.

After she unlocked the door, she stepped inside, leaving him to close the door, and went into the living room to plug in the lights. In the semidarkness the lights turned the tree and its surroundings into a magical scene that invoked all the hopes and dreams of the Christmas season.

He stepped closer, reaching out to touch the glass

ornament he'd given her. "It looks good there, doesn't it?"

Several times Molly had considered taking the ornament down and storing it away. It reminded her of Quinn every time she saw it. She was glad she hadn't done so.

"Yes, it's a beautiful ornament."

He stepped back suddenly, bumping into her. She tried to move away and almost tripped over her long skirt. In the confusion, she found herself wrapped in Quinn's warm embrace. Her hands went to his chest to balance herself, and she stared into his green eyes.

## Chapter Seventeen

Quinn felt her warmth flow through him, heating his body, inflaming his brain. He couldn't help himself. Instead of releasing her, he covered her lips with his.

He promised himself if she rejected him, pushed him away, he'd release her. But she didn't. As before, she opened herself to him, her arms sliding up his chest, wrapping themselves around his neck. He pulled her tighter against him, their bodies touching from lips to knees. Her shawl fell to the floor and his lips traveled down her neck to the promise that waited above the scooped neckline of her gown.

When she moaned, his lips returned to her mouth, wanting to catch that sound, to savor the need she was expressing, to meet it more than halfway. He was rapidly losing control as he touched her soft skin, kissed those full lips. Sliding the shoulder strap down her arm, he bared one breast and immediately kissed her there, gently nibbling at her tight bud, reaching for the other strap.

"Quinn, we shouldn't," she whispered, and he heard the denial in her voice. Quickly he transferred his mouth to hers, to stifle any attempt to withdraw. He couldn't let her go away. He had to have this moment, this taste, because he'd longed for it for too long. It had haunted his nights, denying him sleep. It had filled his days.

When she shoved his overcoat back from his chest, he hurriedly let it slide to the floor. He found the zipper at the back of her dress and released her from its hold, never abandoning her lips. His hands stroked her curves, exulting in their closeness.

As he greedily tasted her, he still had the forethought to move them in the direction of the sofa that faced the Christmas tree. His legs were already growing weak with the power of the attraction. Hell, he'd known it would be like this. He wanted her so badly when she just smiled at him. Touching her lit him up, made it impossible to call a halt to what was happening.

She'd already untied his tie and pulled out the studs on his tuxedo shirt. When her soft hands touched his chest, stroking him as he stroked her, he lowered her to the sofa after lifting her out of the ball gown she'd worn so elegantly.

"Molly," he muttered, unable to think of anything else.

"Too many clothes," she protested, her voice rough, as if in the throes of a high fever.

He divested himself of everything, then did the same for her. He got his wallet out and retrieved a condom at the last minute, to protect Molly, a thought that remained in his head even as he was focused on the exquisite pleasure. Then he lost himself in loving Molly Blake.

WHEN MOLLY LAY SPENT, exhausted by the incredible pleasure of loving Quinn Spencer, she gave thanks. Not because she'd done the right thing, but because, for the first time in her life, she knew what true love was, what sex with the one man she loved more than anyone in the world, except Sara, was like.

And she'd have that memory for the rest of her life.

But she wouldn't have him.

When he'd taken her into his arms, she'd tried to think rationally. But the chemistry they'd tried to deny was too strong. Since she knew Sara was safe, Molly had decided, in a split second, to give herself the gift of loving this man...just once.

A Christmas gift. One that would bring as much pain as ecstasy. But one she'd always have. After Christmas Day, she intended to distance herself from Quinn Spencer.

She moved her hands over his bare back as he lay on top of her, wanting one last touch, one last feeling of his consuming presence, before she sent him away.

As if her touch had awakened him, he lifted his head and kissed her gently, tenderly, making her heart melt again.

"I forgot about Sara," he suddenly whispered. "Do we need to go get her? You said Martha—"

She shook her head and buried her face against his chest. She felt grateful for his consideration of her child. He might leave her, would leave her, but he was a decent man. Something Christopher had never been.

He got up from the sofa, and her heart cried out. *Not yet. Don't leave yet.*

As if he heard her, he didn't reach for his clothes.

Instead, he reached for her, scooping her up against his bare chest.

"Where—"

"To bed, my love. You deserve better treatment than a cold sofa."

Tears seeped from her eyes as she realized she was being given her wish. When he put her down by the entrance to the living room, she wondered if he'd changed his mind. But he leaned over and unplugged the Christmas tree lights, then lifted her against him again.

"I can walk," she whispered, even though she knew they were alone.

"I can't let you go that far away," he said, kissing her again. "I need to feel you against me."

"It's two flights of stairs," she warned, but she snuggled closer to him, feeling the same way.

"There you go again, questioning my manhood," he teased before he lightly kissed her.

Never. She'd known lovemaking with Quinn would be magical, and he'd proven her right. "I just want you to be able to perform," she teased back.

"Damn!" And he set her down again.

"What?" she asked hurriedly, wondering if she'd done something wrong.

Instead of answering, he sprinted back to the living room and grabbed his pants.

Was he going to leave so abruptly? Had he thought she might expect something he couldn't give, in return for their lovemaking?

He held up a gold foil packet and threw his pants on the floor, racing back to her. "I almost forgot." Then he picked her up again and continued up the stairs.

As they reached the top of the second staircase, he said, "It's a good thing you're little or I might not have been able to make it all the way." He paused at the top and kissed her, pulling her tight against him again.

The heat increased, her blood stirring again, desire filling her. "I'd help you," she whispered.

He shoved open the door to her room and rushed to the large bed waiting for them. "I couldn't ask for more," he assured her as he immediately began to make love to her again. Already she responded as if she'd loved him forever, known every inch of his body and still couldn't get enough of him.

As it would always be in her memory. This precious memory would be her own private Christmas dream, one to last her through the years.

WHEN QUINN AWAKENED the next morning, it was early. But he'd slept better, if not longer, than he had in ages.

Than he had since meeting Molly Blake.

He felt her warm body pressed against him and couldn't imagine a better way to start the day. Except by making love with her again. But he'd only carried two condoms with him, and he hadn't bothered to ask Molly if she had any on hand. He already knew the answer to that question.

He could already feel his body stirring against her, and he slid silently away. He wasn't sure he'd have the willpower to protect her.

Besides, as much as he'd loved the incredible sex they'd shared, would share again, he knew he had some decisions to make. He certainly didn't want to face Molly without being able to plan their future. And he couldn't think clearly in her bed.

He quietly went downstairs and dressed in his now wrinkled tux. Then he gathered Molly's gown and undergarments and climbed the stairs again. Just holding her clothes warmed his body. When he saw her sprawled under the cover, one bare shoulder peeking out, he laid her clothes on a chair and got out of there.

Silently he let himself out of the house and paused to draw a deep breath of cold air. Then he realized he'd best get himself and his car out of there before he and Molly became the talk of the town. He knew she'd hate that.

But he stood there a minute longer, not wanting to leave her and break the ties they'd just forged. He wanted to go back to her bed, to never leave it, he realized.

The sound of a car awakened him from his thoughts and he sprinted for the Jeep. The other vehicle turned off on Rose Street, not coming in front of Molly's place, so he eased his car down the driveway and headed for his father's house.

By the time he'd pulled into the driveway at Elias's home, he knew he'd made a mistake. He shouldn't have left her. What would she think when she woke up?

He'd call her. In an hour or two, when she would've awakened. He'd pick her and Sara up to come to his father's. Everything would be all right. He'd explain and…and they'd talk.

Because now he knew what Seth had meant.

He couldn't walk away from Molly and Sara.

MOLLY REALIZED Quinn was leaving when she opened one eye and saw him tiptoeing from her bedroom, dressed in his wrinkled tux.

She didn't move. She didn't want their stolen night, the memory she would cherish, to be tarnished with embarrassed excuses, painful goodbyes.

Instead, she wanted to hold on to his tenderness, his passion…his touch, for a little longer. She wished she could tell him she didn't blame him. He'd made it clear, all along, that he wasn't a forever kind of man. The Spencer men had a reputation. Everyone knew they didn't commit.

He'd been friendly. Helpful. It wasn't his fault that she'd fallen for him. At least, when her beloved Sara came to her to tell her she'd fallen in love, Molly would know what she was experiencing. She'd be able to guide her daughter without bitterness.

Because she wasn't going to be bitter. She'd made her choice. And she didn't regret it.

When she heard the door close downstairs, she slipped from the bed, afraid if she lay there much longer, she'd cry. But she'd had her moment, however brief it had been. She'd loved and been loved…for one night.

She dressed and went downstairs to make a carrot cake with its rich icing for Christmas dinner at the Spencers. Her last time to be close to Quinn Spencer.

WHEN SARA WAS DELIVERED on her doorstep around ten o'clock, Molly led her immediately into the living room, where Santa had left her gifts.

Sara's eyes widened at the doll, resting in a baby carriage. Even as she gathered the doll in her arms, she looked at her mother. "Where's Mr. Spencer?"

Molly's heart thudded. Did Sara know? Had some-one already spread rumors about Quinn spending the night? She sent a silent prayer winging its way up-ward, hoping her selfish greed, letting her spend one night with Quinn Spencer, wouldn't hurt her child.

"What do you mean, Sara? Mr. Spencer is at his house, of course. We're going there for lunch, re-member?"

"Oh," Sara said, her face solemn. "So Santa has gone back to the North Pole?"

Molly wrapped her arms around her child. "I'm afraid so. Did he forget to bring you something you wanted? I thought he did a pretty good job. Did you see the new storybooks? And I saw some puzzles, too, and a game. I know how to play Candyland. Do you want to have a game before we get dressed for lunch?"

Sara smiled and agreed, but Molly got the feeling she was missing something.

They carried the new game to the kitchen and Molly fixed them both cups of hot chocolate, filled with little marshmallows for them to drink. Then they played a game of Candyland.

Sara seemed content, but Molly kept an eye on her. "Do you like this game?" she asked, as they put it away after Sara had won.

"Yes. I want to invite Jeremy over to play it one day."

"That's a good idea. Tonight I'll read you one of your new books before bedtime."

The phone rang. It wasn't the first time it had rung that morning, but Molly had ignored it. She was go-ing to give her daughter one family Christmas at the Spencers, as she'd promised. She figured it was

Quinn calling to cancel her invitation, so she just
didn't answer. She had an answering machine, but
she hadn't connected it yet. It would be a necessity
when she opened her inn, but not today.

"Aren't you going to answer the phone,
Mommy?" Sara asked.

"Not today. It's Christmas. Besides, it's time to
dress to go to the Spencers. Did you see the carrot
cake I made? And I fixed a tray of candy and cookies, too. They're very festive, aren't they?" she asked
brightly.

"What's festive?" Sara asked.

"Um, Christmasy."

"Yes. And our Christmas tree is festive, too, isn't
it? Mr. Spencer really liked it."

So much he'd made love to her under its lights.
But that was a thought for only her to have. Her
memory to cherish.

"Yes, he did. Now let's go put on our party
dresses." Upstairs, after she put Sara in the tub for
her bath, she unplugged the phone. No more phone
calls until Christmas had passed.

Then she got in the shower to wash away any lingering sadness.

QUINN SLAMMED DOWN THE PHONE in frustration.
Where was she? It was after eleven. He'd called
every fifteen minutes for the past several hours. Even
if she'd gone to get Sara, it wouldn't take an hour to
go anywhere in Tyler.

He'd go over there and beat down the door. She
couldn't stay locked up in her ivory tower forever.
He had to talk to her. To tell her he couldn't walk

away. To promise her forever if she'd let him be a part of her and Sara's lives.

"What's wrong, boy?" Elias asked, coming into the hallway.

"Nothing, Dad. I'm going to go over to Molly's and bring her and Sara over."

"Good idea, but there's plenty of time for that. I need you to help me with something."

"Sure," he agreed, but he was straining at the leash to find Molly. He hoped his father's need was brief.

Elias waved for Quinn to follow him up the stairs. In his bedroom, he pointed to a small box sitting on his dresser. "I need some help wrapping that."

Quinn groaned. Then he realized he had the answer. "Hey, why don't you get Jenna to wrap it? She's the artist in the family."

"Damn, I didn't think of that. It's still hard to remember that Seth got himself married, we've all been single for so long."

"Change is in the air," Quinn said, thinking of Molly.

"You're right," Elias agreed, a smile on his face.

"Well, I'll be on my way," Quinn said, edging toward the door.

"Wait a minute. There's one other thing." Elias turned to the closet. Reaching in, he pulled out a Santa suit. "I decided Molly was wrong about Santa. I want to have a Santa for Sara. He can tell her he wants to be sure she got everything she wanted, and to tell her what a good girl she's been. That will work, won't it?"

"I don't know, Dad," Quinn began.

"Besides, I know you put several presents under

the tree for Sara, and Lydia and I got her something, and then, well, there's a present or two for Lydia, and we got presents for Seth and Jenna and Brady. I know they brought some for us. So Santa will have a lot to do.''

Quinn didn't really care about Santa. He wanted to get to Molly. ''Whatever you think,'' he said as he took another step toward the door.

''Good. Try it on.''

Quinn froze. ''What? Me?''

''Of course. Why not?''

''Because Sara will expect me to be there. She'll notice if I'm gone.'' He hoped even more that Molly would notice his absence, but until he talked to her, he couldn't be sure. He shook his head. She couldn't have loved him as she had last night if she hadn't felt something. Molly was too honest. Please, God, let him be right about that.

''Hey, Dad, what are you two doing up here?'' Brady asked, stepping into his father's bedroom.

Quinn seized on his brother's presence. ''Brady can be Santa.''

''What are you talking about? I brought presents, but—''

''I want to have a Santa here for Sara,'' Elias said eagerly. ''We need to think about Christmas in terms of children. After all, next year we'll have a baby to think about,'' Elias explained, his eagerness making it clear how he felt about their growing family.

Brady had a trapped look on his face. ''Well, I think it should be someone Sara's never met. Otherwise, she might figure out he isn't real. She's a smart little girl.''

Quinn kept silent, glad Brady had made sure

Quinn wouldn't be pressured into the role. After all, he knew Sara better than anyone there.

"Cooper!" Elias almost shouted. "He'll be perfect. I don't think he's even met little Sara. Is he here yet? Go get him, Brady."

Again Quinn began edging toward the door, even as he gave a prayer of thanks that Cooper, their long-time friend, always joined them for Christmas dinner. It got him off the hook.

Quinn needed to see Molly, he needed to kiss her under the mistletoe his father had hung yesterday. He needed to hold her close.

"Wait, Quinn. I may need you to help convince Cooper. After all, you know Sara best of all. You can give him some hints about what to say to her."

"Dad, I really need to—"

"Besides, you're not going to wear jeans to our Christmas dinner, are you? I expect better than that."

"No, I'm going to change. In fact, I'll go do that right now."

"Put on something nice," Elias called as Quinn rushed from the room, glad to escape.

He ran into his room and hurriedly changed into navy slacks and a white shirt, topped by a navy sweater with rows of small green fir trees marching across it. His concession to the Christmas season.

After combing his hair, having shaved earlier when he'd showered, he was ready and rushed out of his room, finally on his way to Molly.

And ran into a fat Santa in the hallway.

"Quinn! I was coming to find you," Cooper said, his deep voice in contrast to the jolly picture he presented.

"Later," Quinn protested. "I have to go get Molly and Sara."

"You can't go get Sara until I know what I'm supposed to do. I've never even listened to a department store Santa. How am I supposed to know what they say?" The panic in Cooper Night Hawk's voice would have amused Quinn at any other time. The big, strong deputy sheriff had always seemed confident. But all Quinn could think about was getting to Molly.

"Uh, ask Seth," he suggested, and tried to get by Cooper.

"I did," Cooper protested.

"And I told him I'm new to this stuff, too," Seth said, over Cooper's shoulder.

"Then ask Dad," Quinn shouted, frustration consuming him. "He's a father."

"But he didn't do much about Santa Claus, and you know it, Quinn. We all knew already that the jolly old guy wasn't real. And none of us was in the mood for a happy-ever-after thing." Seth frowned. "I want my baby to have a chance to believe in good things."

"Besides, where are you off to?" Cooper asked. "It's too late to be doing any shopping. What did you get Molly?"

Quinn turned into stone. Nothing. He'd gotten Molly nothing. He wished now he'd found *something* for her. Preferably, an engagement ring. But Coop was right. It was too late for shopping.

"Nothing," he muttered. "We're not—" But they were. They were involved. They were planning a future. But he couldn't tell his brother and his friend that. Because he hadn't told—asked Molly yet.

"Nothing?" Seth asked, raising his eyebrows. "You should've gotten her something," he protested. "Maybe Dad bought her a gift." He turned around and disappeared into his father's bedroom. Quinn could hear the deep timbre of his voice.

"Do you know what Sara got for Christmas?" Cooper asked, still worried about his role.

"Molly said once that she was getting a doll and some storybooks. I'll ask her as soon as I go pick them up."

"You're picking them up? I thought they were driving over. When she talked to Lydia a few minutes ago—"

Quinn reached out and grabbed the front of the Santa suit. "She talked to Lydia?" he demanded, frowning fiercely.

"Yeah, just as I arrived," Cooper said, his eyebrows raised.

Quinn didn't care what Cooper thought about his behavior. He shoved past him and ran down the stairs to the kitchen, even as Cooper yelled for him to come back and answer his questions.

Quinn burst into the kitchen. "Lydia? Did you talk to Molly?"

Lydia, stirring something on the stove, looked up, surprised. "Why, yes, I did. Why?"

"When? When did she call? Where was she? Is she still coming? When was she leaving?"

Jenna was tossing dressing into a big salad, but she stopped and stared at him. "Can you put those questions in order? And explain what's going on?"

Quinn waved a hand toward her, dismissing her smiling demands. "Lydia?"

"Well, let's see. She was at home. She said they

were almost ready and would be leaving in a few minutes. She wanted to know if she should bring anything else. What was your other question?''

Even Quinn had trouble remembering exactly what he'd asked. As he frantically paused to think, Jenna said, "I think he wanted to know exactly when she'd called. I think it was when we were checking on the turkey, about fifteen minutes ago."

"Yes, that's right," Lydia said, beaming at him.

"Damn!" he muttered. He must've just gone up the stairs with his father. He strode to the kitchen phone and quickly dialed her number. It rang and rang. No answering machine. No nothing. Just as it had been all morning.

He checked his watch. It was almost twelve. If he went to find her, he could miss her and she'd arrive without him there to greet her. To hurry her off somewhere where they could be private. Where he could ask her—

"What's going on?" Elias asked as he entered the kitchen.

"We don't know," Lydia said. "Quinn seems upset about something."

"He'll get over it," Elias said with a chuckle. "Uh, Jenna, could I see you for a minute?"

"Well, I have to finish fixing the salad," she said, staring at the huge bowl.

"Quinn can do that. Take care of the salad, son, while I borrow Jenna for a moment."

He winked at Quinn, and Quinn bowed his head in acquiescence. He might as well help out. He'd have to wait until Molly arrived. She'd be there any minute.

"What was that all about?" Lydia asked when only the two of them remained in the kitchen.

He didn't know if she was asking about his questions or his father's abduction of Jenna. Either way, he didn't have an answer.

# Chapter Eighteen

Molly was dressed in her royal-blue sweaterdress that she'd worn at the open house, and Sara was in her green taffeta.

"I like our new dresses, Mommy," Sara said as she sat beside Molly in the car.

"Yes, sweetie, and you look wonderful. Do you have Jeremy's present?"

To insure they didn't arrive early at the Spencers', she'd told Sara they would delivery Jeremy's present to him on the way.

By the time Sara and Jeremy exchanged their presents and they left the Kelseys', it was almost twelve-thirty.

They definitely wouldn't be early.

She'd prefer that they arrive just as everyone was sitting down to eat. She didn't want any private confrontations with Quinn. Though she longed to see him. And touch him.

"Are we almost there, Mommy?"

"Yes, sweetie, we are," she said as she turned into the driveway at the stately mansion where Elias and Quinn lived. "In fact, we *are* here. Remember to use your best manners,'' she added as Sara undid her seat belt.

She slid the large tray of cookies and candy out of the back seat and guided Sara to the back door, where she suspected the kitchen was located.

Jenna and Lydia were both there.

"There you are!" Lydia exclaimed. "Quinn has been going crazy looking for you."

She'd been right. He didn't want her there and had been trying to tell her to stay away. Molly tightened her lips and raised her chin. "Sorry if we're late."

"Oh, you're not late," Jenna assured her. "The guys are in the living room gobbling up hors d'oeuvres, and I'm going to kill them if they don't leave any room for turkey. Go on in and visit."

Molly set down her tray. "I also have a cake in the car. I'll go get it first. I'll be back in a minute, Sara," she assured her child, and hurried out the back door.

When she came back in with the cake, she didn't see Sara. "Where—"

"I told her to go on in," Lydia said. "She was reluctant to until I reminded her that Quinn was in there."

Molly hurried to the door, anxious to check on her child, just as she heard a shriek. She began to run.

When she reached the doorway to the living room, Quinn was in the middle of the room, heading her way. But Sara had already discovered a special guest.

"Mommy! Mommy, he's here. He hasn't gone home yet!" Sara shouted, absolute joy in her voice.

Though she was distracted by Quinn's intense stare and his hands reaching out for her, Molly turned her attention to Sara. She discovered her sitting on the knee of a Santa who was anything but a jolly old soul.

"Santa's here. And he's got more presents for me." Sara's little face beamed with anticipation. "I bet it's the one I asked for. I just know it!"

Molly's heart clutched. She'd known this morning that something was missing from Sara's Christmas, but she hadn't figured out what. She hoped she was wrong about her guess now.

Quinn had reached her side and taken hold of her arm, but he, too, turned to face Sara. "What did you ask for that he didn't bring you, sweetheart?"

Sara slipped off Santa's lap and raced across the room to throw her arms around his legs. "You! I asked him for you to be my daddy. Mommy said it was all right to wish for it, but she said it couldn't happen. But Santa can do anything." As if remembering her manners, her eyes rounded, she spun on her heel and raced back across the room to reach up and hug Santa's neck. "Thank you, Santa. I love you!" Then she raced back to Quinn and Molly.

Molly thought she'd die a thousand deaths. And none would be so torturous as knowing she'd failed her child so completely. She should have found a way to refuse the invitation. She should've taken Quinn's call this morning and opted out of the dinner. She should've never let Quinn Spencer into her heart.

Silent tears slid down her cheeks and she knelt to embrace her child. "Baby, Santa can't— It's not true. Remember," she said, sniffing back the tears, but they were falling faster than she could control them. "Remember, we're a team, you and me. It's just the two of us. That's all it will ever be. Quinn can't—''

A strong arm tugged her to her feet and she turned a fierce glare his way.

''I think I can speak for myself,'' Quinn assured her.

''Don't hurt her,'' she pleaded in a whisper.

Quinn knelt and picked up Sara. Her little face had lost its glow and she stared at her mother's tears. He whispered in Sara's ear, and the glow, the smile returned. Then she leaned toward Molly and hugged her.

Before Molly could respond, shocked at the rapid change in her daughter, Quinn had set Sara down and she was running back to Santa.

''What did you say?'' she demanded, anger rising in her. He'd made false promises to her daughter. She couldn't believe she'd trusted this man, given herself to him, because she thought he was a decent man, because she thought he loved Sara, because she loved him.

''Excuse us, folks,'' Quinn said, a smile almost as brilliant as Sara's on his lips. ''Molly and I have something to discuss.''

''No! No, I have to leave. We have to—''

He didn't give her a chance to finish. Scooping her up into his arms, as he'd done last night to go to her bedroom, he walked out of the living room.

She struggled against his hold, afraid if she didn't she'd forget that she was breaking Sara's heart. ''Put me down! We have nothing to discuss. How could you hurt Sara like that?''

''The only one who will hurt Sara is you, Molly, if you turn down my proposal.''

Stunned, afraid to believe she'd heard correctly, she stared at him and said nothing. He slid her down his body in the hallway and covered her lips with his in an all-consuming kiss that reminded her of their embraces the night before.

She tried to summon her control, to resist his touch, to clear her head and deny the hope that rose in her. "You can't—" she said as he lifted his lips from her.

"I not only can, I'll die if I don't," he muttered, and kissed her again.

A kiss so gentle, so tender, so committed, she almost believed her dreams would come true. When he stopped kissing her this time, she buried her face in his sweater and sobbed, "Don't."

"Don't kiss you? Don't hold you?" He took a deep breath. "Or don't ever let you go?" He bent and kissed her neck. "Because the last one is the only one I can agree to."

She shoved against him and lifted her head. "But you don't want forever. And I can't let you hurt Sara that way."

"Oh, but I do. And I love Sara with all my heart and I don't want to hurt her. But what about you? How does forever sound to you?"

She sobbed and hid against him again. "Quinn, I'm not teasing."

"Neither am I, Molly. I left this morning because I didn't have any more condoms. And because I wanted to be sure about everything before I faced you again. I knew I'd made a mistake by the time I left your house. Leaving was wrong."

She nodded, but she didn't lift her head.

"I tried to call all morning."

"I thought you were calling to ask me not to come," she confessed.

"I'm encouraged that you wanted to see me."

She looked up then, tragedy on her face. "I wanted to see you one more time, to touch you, to— to remember. I knew you didn't want—"

He stopped her with another shattering kiss. Then he said, "Oh, but I do. With all my heart, all my life, forever and ever. I can't live without you and Sara. Please say you'll give Sara her Christmas wish. Tell me you'll give me a chance to be the best husband and daddy there is."

Molly raised her hand to stroke his cheek. "I want that more than anything, Quinn, but are you sure?"

"More sure than I've ever been." He kissed her again, a kiss full of promise, of love, of Christmas.

"Now let's go inform our daughter that she must've been extra good this year, since Santa brought her exactly what she wished for."

There was a collective gasp when they entered the living room again, all eyes focused on them. Sara, who had again occupied Santa's knee, slid down from her perch and stared at them.

"Sara, my girl, I'm your special Christmas present," Quinn announced, a big smile on his face. "But you have to promise to share me with Mommy. Okay?"

Sara rushed to them again, the glow firmly in place, and everyone in the room gave a cheer as a new family was born on Christmas Day.

# Epilogue

"Molly?" Quinn called up the stairway. "Are you ready? I promised Martha we'd be there at two."

When she appeared above him, he again gave thanks that she—and Sara—were going to be a part of his life forever. He still couldn't believe how fortunate he'd been. Though every time he took her in his arms, he was believing a little more.

"I'm ready. Why did Martha want us to come today? With the wedding tomorrow and the opening in two weeks, things are kind of hectic," she added as she ran down the stairs.

"You know you've got everything under control," he pointed out. "After all, if you weren't so efficient, I wouldn't have bought in as a partner."

He'd insisted he put some of his own money into Molly's business. He wanted to share in every aspect of her life.

"Oh, is that so?" she responded, grinning just as much as him. "I don't remember discussing my efficiency."

"Well, no, you distracted me. I'd never negotiated a contract before without my clothes on." Even thinking about the times they'd managed to make love, when Sara was out of the house, brought pleasure. It hadn't happened often enough. But after tomorrow, he'd have the right to hold Molly in his arms every night.

"I'd say you should try it more often," she teased back, "but I don't want you naked with anyone but me."

"Me, neither," he assured her, gathering her close.

"We're late, remember?" she said after he kissed her. Her breathing was a little erratic, like his, which pleased him.

Reluctantly he took her hand and headed out the door.

When they reached the room in Worthington House where the ladies quilted, they discovered the quilting loom put away and a table covered with a dainty cloth and a vase of flowers in its place.

"What's this? You've given up quilting?" Quinn teased as they entered.

"Of course not," Martha said with a smile. "We couldn't do that, don't you know. But today is special."

Lydia stepped forward and took Molly's hand. "Come sit down, you two. We have something for you."

Quinn had figured what was coming, but his darling Molly seemed to have no idea.

"It's a tradition here in Tyler," Martha said, the other ladies nodding in agreement, "to present newlyweds with their very own quilt. It's a special treat, Molly, my dear, to give one to you and Quinn. You appreciate our work so much. And you're marrying one of our favorite people." She beamed at Quinn.

"Oh, Martha! You've all done so much work for

me,'' Molly protested. ''You shouldn't have gone to so much trouble.''

Martha replied, ''It was a labor of love, my dear.''

Quinn put his arms around Molly and smiled at all the ladies. ''And so is our marriage, ladies. We're going to have a patchwork family to rival the beauty and endurance of the patchwork quilts of Tyler.''

And he kissed Molly while the Quilting Circle cheered.

\* \* \* \* \*

*Watch for more Tyler stories
in a special anthology—TYLER BRIDES.
This collection of romances is set in
Molly's B & B and is available
from Harlequin Books this January.*

*And be sure to look for another
RETURN TO TYLER story from
Harlequin American Romance,
this February with
PRESCRIPTION FOR SEDUCTION,
by Darlene Scalera.*

# Tyler Brides

### It happened one weekend...

Quinn and Molly Spencer are delighted to accept three
bookings for their newly opened B&B, Breakfast Inn Bed,
located in America's favorite hometown, Tyler, Wisconsin.

But Gina Santori is anything but thrilled to discover her
best friend has tricked her into sharing a room with
the man who broke her heart eight years ago....

And Delia Mayhew can hardly believe that she's
gotten herself locked in the Breakfast Inn Bed
basement with the sexiest man in America.

Then there's Rebecca Salter. She's turned up at the
Inn in her wedding gown. Minus her groom.

*Come home to Tyler for three delightful novellas
by three of your favorite authors: Kristine Rolofson,
Heather MacAllister and Jacqueline Diamond.*

HARLEQUIN®
*Makes any time special* ™

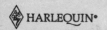

# TEXAS CONFIDENTIAL

Penny Archer has always been the
dependable and hardworking executive
assistant for Texas Confidential, a secret
agency of Texas lawmen. But her daring
heart yearned to be the heroine of her
own adventure—and to find a love
that would last a lifetime.

And this time...

## THE SECRETARY GETS HER MAN
by Mindy Neff

Coming in January 2001 from

 HARLEQUIN®

AMERICAN *Romance*

If you missed the TEXAS CONFIDENTIAL series
from Harlequin Intrigue, you can place an order
with our Customer Service Department.

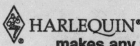

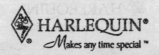

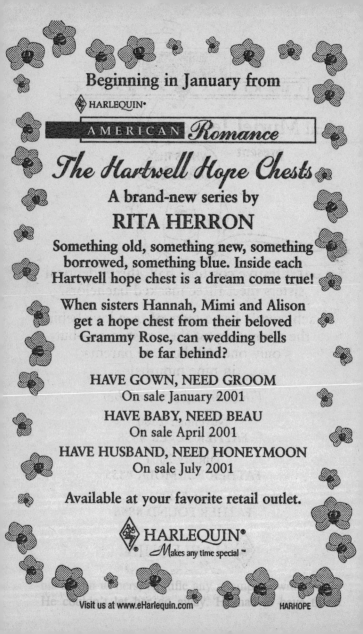